LUCKY FOR LOVE

BY

MARINA OLIVER

See details of other books by Marina Oliver at
http:/www.marina-oliver.net.

Published by Marina Oliver

ISBN: 978-1-326-79125-4

Author Note

I've been lucky enough to do several lecture cruises on luxury ships, and always meant to set a romance on one. Most cruises last around two weeks, so the progression of any romance has to be swift, the attraction immediate, and opportunities for development frequent. One meets entertaining, interesting, and sometimes odd characters, amongst passengers and crew. As a guest lecturer I was privy to some of the behind the scenes activity as well as being with the passengers.

Chapter 1

'You need a break, a holiday, but one where you'll meet people, not sit in a hotel room on your own, pining,' Susan Phillips had declared.

Julie Carstairs suppressed a grin. Susan was still the same bossy elder sister she had been in her teens, but it would be useless to tell her so. If she pretended to listen Susan would probably forget it by next week. And she didn't pine all the time. Not every day, at least.

'You mean some sort of residential course?' Julie Carstairs asked. 'I tried that last year, and just came to the conclusion I had absolutely no talent for either sketching or painting. No thanks, it simply made me feel utterly useless.'

Susan was impatient. 'Not that sort of break. I am suggesting a cruise, that's what you should do. And if you came with me you wouldn't be alone, even though I'm working on the ship.'

'Me? A cruise? But Susan, surely only old people, pensioners, go on cruises?'

Susan laughed. 'You're out of touch, Julie. Not these days. We even have children, but not many, and it's not holiday time. Some of the bigger ships have special facilities, crêches and playgroups, but thank goodness our ship is one of the small ones, and we haven't gone that far.'

'I'll think about it.' That would shut Susan up. She had thought about it, for an hour or two, and dismissed the idea. It didn't sound like her at all.

*

Robert Fellows glanced up from the papers he was reading, and across the aisle towards the girl in the first seat. He didn't seem able to stop looking at her. It wasn't just her looks. She was pretty, with her dark auburn curly hair and pale face, but nothing like as beautiful as the red-haired girl seated next to him, or Lucy, who had changed his life six years ago. Yet something about her attracted his attention. Perhaps it was the slight droop to her

5

shoulders, the resigned attitude he detected in her down-turned lips, but most of all the wistfulness he'd seen in her clear green eyes when she happened to glance towards him for a moment.

She'd looked straight through him, it had seemed, as though her thoughts were far away, and not very pleasant ones at that. It was not the sort of expression to be expected of someone setting off on holiday in the south of Spain. Most of the other passengers seemed to be looking forward to a time in the sun. Some of them, no doubt, would be heading for a cruise ship, others driving off to hotels and villas along the Costa del Sol. It wasn't the height of the holiday season, but the plane was full. Plenty of Brits thought two weeks in Spain's winter sun, or on a luxury cruise to the Canaries preferable to the cold in England.

He shook his head to clear it. He had no time to waste wondering about the sorrows of a stranger, and no interest in women since he'd lost Lucy. He had a job to do, one which needed his full concentration, and if he didn't manage to solve the mystery in the next two weeks the police would have to be brought in, with all the bad publicity for the firm that would produce. But he couldn't resist looking to see whether she wore a wedding ring, and was oddly cheered to see she didn't. Her only ring was a deep green emerald worn on her right hand. Emeralds, he recalled, implied wisdom and love, and to give a lover an emerald made them faithful. It was a symbol of hope. Well, that remained to be tested.

*

Julie sat hunched in her seat. She'd refused the plastic lunch offering, apart from a tiny cup of coffee, and was wishing she hadn't allowed Susan, on a few days off while the cruise ship she worked on underwent a minor overhaul, to hustle her into coming. Susan hadn't permitted her time to think, but then Susan never did stop to think herself, she was far more impulsive than Julie had ever been. If she'd had longer to consider it she'd have been stronger, and refused. It had been the anniversary of Andrew's death, and she'd been vulnerable, so when Susan produced

6

photographs of the ship and itineraries, and talked about the facilities and the many wonderful places it called at, she had shrugged and agreed, so here they were, starting off from Malaga and heading for the Canaries, with a final stop in Casablanca. It had been easier to let her sister have her own way, and make all the arrangements.

Though she was committed now Julie still wasn't at all sure about this holiday, but then, she hadn't been sure of much for ages. Two years ago she'd thought she was at last getting over her loss, even beginning to open her mind to the possibility of happiness once more, and then it had all fallen apart again.

She took a deep breath. She must shake off this negative attitude, she had to try and enjoy herself, if only for Susan's sake. It was only for two weeks, and on the bright side was the fact she would not have to cook. Devising interesting meals for one was usually too much trouble, and she normally ended up with something on toast, or a freezer meal. At least on the ship she'd have plenty of choice, and from the sample menus Susan had displayed, things she didn't normally taste unless she went out with friends. She could make the big decisions she'd been putting off for months when she got back to England.

She could hear Susan chattering to the woman in the window seat. From the occasional words she caught it seemed as though the woman was a fellow passenger, but one who had never before been on a cruise. Susan was reassuring her that the ship was stable, she wouldn't feel the movement, and she need not worry about being on her own.

'There are plenty of other singles,' Susan said. 'You'll soon meet people to talk to. And if you play bridge there are regular games. Why, there are even men to dance with.'

The woman laughed, and said her dancing days were long over, but she did play bridge.

Julie stopped listening. She wondered whether Susan was expecting her to talk to other passengers, to bare her soul, perhaps? She shook her head slightly. She'd resolutely avoided talking about herself and her feelings after Andrew died, even to friends, apart from that one occasion when she had let her guard drop, and what a disaster that had been. It had only reawakened the agony she'd thought was beginning to lessen.

Well, she could relax in the sun. And there would be the various stops where she could try to forget, though perhaps seeing the places she and Andrew had intended to visit one day might not be the best way to forget how life had treated her.

She firmly told herself brooding was useless. Susan was right, it was time she made decisions, got on with her life. Should she sell the house and move to a different town, start again where no one knew her, instead of remaining where people either avoided the subject or told her to snap out of it and find another man? She didn't want another man, and recalling her friends' occasional well-meaning introductions to eligible males made her alternately laugh at their ideas of the sort of men she might like, or become annoyed they might believe she could fall in love with such confirmed bachelors or predatory divorced men looking for someone to minister to their creature comforts. She hadn't been attracted to any of them. They were either the nerdy types who hadn't bothered to find a girl friend, or the brash, over-confident ones on their second or even third divorces. She had no desire to change the first, nor become a notch on the others' bedposts.

Yet, a wayward thought intruded, would she refuse if, say, a man like the one seated across the aisle showed any interest in her? He was tall and dark, and his profile as good as any she'd seen on TV. The typical romantic tall dark and handsome hero. Once she had glanced across to find him looking directly at her, and had been slightly shocked by the intent look in his eyes. Deep-set, grey eyes fringed with impossibly long and thick lashes. Any girl would die for those, she'd thought before turning away. But she kept thinking about him. Early thirties, she judged. Was he married to the gorgeous red-head seated next to him? She'd had the impression he'd been talking to her and the older woman in the window seat beyond her. A man like him had to be married.

8

He couldn't have reached his age without some girl finding him. She couldn't see his ring finger, but what would that prove? Not all men wore wedding rings. Besides, he was so gorgeous he was bound to be arrogant, for he would have silly women falling over each other to attract his attention.

She shook her head at her wayward thoughts. What was she doing, thinking in such terms about a complete stranger? Susan was right, she needed to get a life. It was time to let go of the past. She twisted her ring. When he'd given it to her on their first anniversary Andrew had said emeralds were lucky for love, and brought tranquillity. She must, she decided, make more of an effort to help the emerald. It couldn't bring Andrew back, but when she got back home she would make some changes. Exactly what she didn't know, but maybe during this next fortnight she could start to think about it, make plans, and acquire some peace.

*

'Please remain seated until the plane has come to a halt,' the pilot intoned, but many of the passengers in aisle seats ignored him. They were standing up to open the lockers, locate their bags and be first off the plane.

'Though why they bother when we only have to wait for our main luggage,' Susan said, glaring at an offending man from the row in front, who oozed fat and was dressed in shorts and a scruffy tee shirt. 'Why didn't we come on a regular flight instead of charter?'

Julie put back her head and closed her eyes. 'You arranged it. Don't fret, big sister.'

A moment later she felt her shoulder jolted and looked up in annoyance to see the man who'd occupied the seat across the aisle from her clutching a bag which had fallen from the opened locker. It was inches from her head.

'Watch what you're doing!' she said furiously, shaking from shock. 'That could have brained me!'

Then she realised her mistake as the man, raising his eyebrows slightly, handed the bag to the fat man in shorts and turned away.

9

She bit her lip. 'I'm sorry,' she muttered, embarrassed. He must have moved remarkably swiftly to catch the bag and save her a nasty bump, or even worse injury. He gave a brief nod, and reached up to the locker opposite to hand down bags to the women sitting beside him.

He wore a lightweight grey suit, beautifully cut, fitting him perfectly. He looked more like a businessman than a tourist, though his shoulders were broad and his hips narrow, muscles rippling beneath the jacket.

Julie had a mental vision of him in swimming trunks, and blinked hard. What was the matter with her? She didn't react like this to men, even when they looked like movie stars. She never had, except to Andrew, and that one dreadful mistake since.

The sisters waited until the gangway was clear before collecting their own hand baggage, and Susan chuckled as their cases appeared on the carousel while the fat man was still waiting, dancing from one foot to the other with impatience.

'Serve the fat slob right. I hope to goodness he's not with us. He doesn't look the cruising type, somehow. I bet he's off to the nearest beach where he can find English beer and fried breakfasts.'

Julie had been looking about her, trying to locate the man who had caught the bag, but he'd vanished. She wanted to apologise, and thank him more gracefully than the first time. Either he'd been exceptionally lucky and his bag had arrived at once, or he travelled light with only hand luggage.

As they went outside she saw him standing by the edge of the pavement, with the women who'd been sitting by him. Both of them were slim and elegantly dressed. His wife and her mother, she wondered? There was a slight resemblance, though the older woman's hair was brown, not flaming red.

Just then a taxi drew to a halt beside them, but before they could climb in the fat man, followed by an equally fat woman wearing a tight tee shirt and tight spangle-scattered jeans, had rushed up and opened the boot, and begun to fling in several cases. Julie felt her hackles rise. He was even more of a mannerless boor than his appearance suggested.

To her amused satisfaction the other man stepped forward, and calmly removed the bags. Julie was too far away to hear the exchange, but after waving his arms about in a threatening manner, the fat one shrugged, piled his bags back onto the trolley, and dashed across to another taxi. The women, who had been standing back during the altercation, climbed in the taxi. Julie was not sure, but she thought he bent down and kissed the red-head. Then he stepped back and waved to them as the taxi departed.

So he wasn't with them. Julie experienced a moment of satisfaction, and chided herself. What did it matter to her? She'd never meet him again. Not unless he was on the return flight, she thought, and blushed. She didn't fantasise about men like this, even when they were handsome and elegant. Especially not when they were handsome and elegant! Then he hailed another taxi, climbed in and was whisked away.

She felt an odd sense of loss. She'd certainly never see him again unless he was booked on the same cruise, but if so, why wasn't he waiting for the buses that were to take them to the docks? It wasn't likely such a man would go on a cruise. She must get a grip. She didn't want a man, with all the complications it would cause.

*

'This is a horrible mistake,' she said an hour later, gritting her teeth as the coach jolted over a bump in the road. 'I shouldn't have let you persuade me to come.'

Susan, smaller and darker than Julie, equally slim, her puckish face surrounded by dark curly hair, grinned at her. 'Cheer up, we'll soon be on the boat, and then it will be different, I promise. You'll see.'

Julie frowned. Would it? She'd only been away from home on a proper holiday once, a year after Andrew died, when Susan had persuaded her she had to stop mourning and had taken her to stay in a villa rented with some friends. That had ended in disaster when she'd made an utter fool of herself.

She stared out at the scrubby hillside festooned with pastel-painted villas, and tried to forget. It was the similarity of the country, the seaside, the shimmering heat, the aromatic scents drifting down from the hills that brought back these unpleasant memories.

'Why don't we go straight to the boat? I wonder if that man who sat by us on the flight and took the taxi knew what we were in for? Oh, but I suppose he could be going somewhere else.' She really must stop thinking about him. 'Why this pointless trip along the Costa whatever it is?'

The woman across the aisle grinned sympathetically at her.

'It often happens. The flight has to be early, to take back the ones who've finished their holidays, and they aren't ready for us on the boat. They need time for the changeover.'

Julie nodded. It was turning out as frustrating as she'd expected.

'So they send us off to some Spanish seaside resort for a couple of hours, when all I want is to unpack and put my feet up.'

Susan laughed. 'Cheer up, sis. At least it isn't high season, so the place won't be crawling with Brits and kids. October's still warm, and we can indulge in a gin and tonic. That'll cheer you up.'

Julie subsided, laid her head back against the seat, and closed her eyes. There was no point in complaining and upsetting Susan. She still wished she hadn't allowed her sister to bully her into this trip, but it was done now. She could either endure it, or make some effort and try to enjoy it. She and Andrew had never been cruising. And now he never would.

A tear squeezed its way between her eyelids, and she surreptitiously wiped it away with her finger. This was ridiculous. Andrew had been dead for three years. She'd thought she was recovering. Never forgetting, she told herself hurriedly, but the pain and the shock of his sudden death had begun to grow less sharp.

She felt Susan clasp her hand, and took a deep breath. Her sister loved her and, as she had from a child, wanted to look after her.

'Sorry,' she whispered. 'I'll stop moaning, promise.'

Susan had probably been right, she admitted at last. She did
need some distraction. The house had been unbearable, she had
rattled round in its emptiness, with every single room and every
item of furniture and all the things they had chosen together
reminding her of Andrew. Ought she to move to somewhere
smaller? Would leaving the house where they had been so happy
ease the constant pain of memories? She really would decide after
this holiday was over. Her sister had known she needed to get
away.

*

Three hours later Julie stood on the quayside looking up at the
elegant ship. Already her spirits had lifted. She'd actually enjoyed
walking round the small village where the coach had deposited
them, exploring the old part, wandering through the narrow
streets, often connected with flights of steps. The houses were
decorated with elaborate iron balconies, flowers bloomed
everywhere, and in every tiny open square there were pavement
cafés. The weather helped too. It was much warmer than in damp,
cold England, with a gentle westerly breeze bringing wafts of
aromatic scents down from the hillsides. Now, in the harbour, the
smells were of fish and oil, less pleasant than flowers and the
open sea, but she suddenly felt excitement building up inside her.

The crew were carrying on the luggage, and the passengers were
being checked off by the tour rep before boarding, queueing at the
desk for keys, and being directed to their cabins.

'I'm allowed to share with you,' Susan told her. 'Normally I'd
share with either Cathy or Debbie, the other shop assistants, but as
you have a double cabin and the ship's not full, I managed to
arrange it. I thought you'd prefer not being on your own.'

'Of course,' Julia agreed.

What did it matter? Susan would be busy working much of the
time, there would be plenty of time for her to hide away in
solitude if she wished. Then she shook her head slightly,
reminding herself she'd made a resolution to change her life. She

ought to start right now.

Susan took charge, and their keys were handed over to a tall man wearing a track suit emblazoned with the ship's name.

Julie looked at him properly and gasped. It was the good-looking man from the plane.

'You were on the plane,' she exclaimed before she could stop herself, then blushed as she realised she had given away the fact she had paid attention to him.

'Yes. I remember you. Mrs Carstairs, Miss Phillips, welcome aboard.'

Julie felt herself flushing.

'You caught that bag, and saved me a nasty bump. I didn't say thank you properly, I was taken by surprise. I'm sorry I snapped at you. I thought it was your bag.'

'Understandable in the circumstances. Don't worry, I was glad to be of help. Please come this way,' he directed, taking their hand luggage and turning into a wide passageway. His voice was pleasant, deep and resonant. He could probably sing.

She was at it again, imagining things about him. This had to stop, before she did something silly.

'Is he crew or what? That must be why he came straight to the ship,' Julie whispered as they followed him. His shoulders were broad, and he looked in great physical shape. Did they have fitness instructors on board? She could imagine him as one of them.

Susan shrugged. 'Could be anyone. I haven't seen him before, but then, people move around all the time, go on different ships. I'm only here permanently because the shop is a concession and I'm employed by Cathy, not the cruise line. They rope in all the waiters and stewards and chefs and whatever to help with the luggage on changeover days.'

Then he turned and indicated their cabin, smiling down at them. Julie was able to take a closer look at him. He had an interesting face, as handsome as her previous quick glances had determined, with strong bone structure and deep laughter creases round the eyes. He was tanned, so had probably been aboard a ship for months. If, as seemed likely from what Susan said, he worked for the cruise line, he'd spend his life sailing in sunny climes.

What was his job? Susan said the whole crew were roped in to move the luggage. Was he a waiter? Somehow she didn't think so. Nor did he look like a chef. They, surely, spent most of their time inside, but his tan indicated an outdoor life. Maybe he was one of the officers. The clothes he'd been wearing on the plane had been expensive, definitely not a ready-to-wear suit. He had to earn more than a chef or a waiter to afford that. Then she frowned. What did it matter?

*

Chapter 2

Robert, having helped with the luggage, made his way to the Captain's office near the bridge. He wondered about Mrs Carstairs. She hadn't been wearing a wedding ring, and he had felt a jolt of unexpected dismay to hear her married name. Why was she on her own? Was she divorced? Widowed? Then he told himself to stop thinking about her. He had a job to do. Besides, if he wished, he had two weeks to get to know her. And somehow he knew he did want to get to know her, find out what caused the melancholy look in her eyes.

'I've read the reports,' he said, sinking down into a chair beside the Captain's desk. 'Is there anything more you can tell me?'

'I don't think so.' The Captain nodded towards the file Robert had placed on his desk. 'You have it all there.'

'Then to recap, these thefts, of money and jewellery, things easily hidden, have only taken place from the penthouse suites. Where the pickings could be better than elsewhere.'

The Captain nodded. 'Where our wealthiest passengers are. But if news of this gets out, if the police are involved, we'll lose a lot of bookings.'

'The engineers, the chefs, and most of the cabin stewards don't have access there, so can be disregarded. How sure are you of that?'

'They would be noticed. We always have at least one security guard stationed up there. But the suites have to be cleaned, and waiters and bar staff may be called on, though we have checked all these people after a theft has been reported. We've moved them elsewhere, even to other ships, so they don't have access to the suites. But the thefts continue. I think we can discount them.'

'You'll keep it so that only new people have access?'

'We've done that for the past three cruises, but the thefts have continued,' the Captain said with a sigh.

'Who else goes to these suites?'

'There are private parties when some of the others of the crew,

16

the entertainers, for instance, or the sports instructors, are invited. Some of these passengers rarely stir from the suites. They eat there, have their own balconies, and just occasionally come out for the shows or to play bridge or go into the casino.'

'Yet some have parties? They are not all segregating themselves?'

'Some are more gregarious, yes, but in general they prefer small, exclusive affairs. Occasionally we have one who expects the pianist or other musicians to give them a private concert. And they scour the passenger lists to invite, say, anyone with a title or a military rank. And they ask the senior officers. Some of the passengers have got rich and want to mix with the upper classes, boast about the celebrities they've met when they get home. We've had a couple of lottery winners like that. Pure snobbishness.'

Robert nodded. 'It has to be someone who has been on board for the past three months, from the time the first theft was reported. Can you trust all the officers?'

The Captain looked offended.

'Yes, of course. I know all of them well, they've worked with me for years.'

'But none of them have been transferred to other ships?'

'Well, no. I can trust them.'

'Can I have a list of all the crew members?'

The Captain passed across a sheaf of papers stapled together.

'Rather a lot, I'm afraid. We have a high ratio of crew to passengers, as you know.'

Robert left it at that. He would have to investigate the officers. It wasn't unknown for someone high up in the ranking order to be a crook.

'You've cleared the stewards, for instance? They have the most opportunity, of course.'

'We've moved them around, none have worked there for more than a month at a time, and after a theft they have been moved, and we have discreetly searched their belongings, so I think we can disregard them.'

'Probably. But these searches could mean the rest of the crew are aware of the thefts.'

'Unfortunately, so though we try to do it without their knowledge, they can know what we are doing, so will be extra careful. And we can eliminate anyone who has joined us after the first theft. I have a separate list of them and the dates they joined, so I think we can forget them.'

He handed over more papers.

'Unless there are two or more working together,' Robert said. 'Who joined roughly three months ago?'

Yet another list was handed over.

'I see how these people are the obvious suspects, but of course, whoever it is might not have been stealing before then, or a theft may not have been reported, so we can't discount people on board beforehand,' the Captain said.

'And it's possible, if only small amounts of cash were stolen, sometimes people may not have noticed, or been too embarrassed to report they'd been careless. Maybe the thief got bolder if the first thefts were unnoticed.'

The Captain groaned.

'That simply makes it more complicated. But we don't want to call in the police if we can avoid it. Think of the international complications, them investigating in several jurisdictions, whatever the law of the sea says. That's why you're here.'

'Our last chance before we have to make it official.'

'Then I wish you luck. We've tried to make a list of all the people we know who have been up to the penthouse suites to parties, but it's far from complete. Here it is.'

Robert looked at the several sheets of paper he had acquired.

'Are these lists on a computer? It would make checking them against one another simpler.'

'They are on my machine. Use it whenever you like.'

He handed over another list.

'And of course,' he said, 'when most of these people go there, the passengers will be present, so it needs some sleight of hand as well as a careless passenger leaving things on view, for them to help themselves.'

Robert glanced at the latest list. It was headed with the names of the regular entertainers, the dancers and musicians, then people like fitness trainers, masseurs, hairdressers, shop girls – most of them people who usually worked on ships for several months. Alongside the names were dates when they had been known to visit one of the suites, but as the Captain, said, this was far from a complete record.

They discussed the thefts for another quarter of an hour, then Robert went to his own cabin. He had not told the Captain of the special measures he had put in place for himself. The less anyone knew of those the more chance there was of trapping the thief.

*

Julie's mood had improved. She was here, she might as well try to enjoy the luxury. She was delighted with the cabin, and when their big cases arrived she unpacked swiftly and stowed their belongings in the drawers and wardrobe, while Susan lay on the bunk reading a letter which had been left for her. Julie exclaimed at the clever use of small spaces, then pushed her suitcase into the bottom of the wardrobe.

'Let's go and explore,' she said, picking up the leaflet which she'd found on the dressing table. 'I can't follow these deck diagrams. I need to see them.'

Susan shook her head.

'You go. I have to start work. This is from Cathy, and she needs me as soon as possible to help her deal with new goods in the shop, and see what she has bought. We try to stock a few different goods each cruise, and we'll have to find space for them before we open later this evening.'

'Why so late?'

'We're not allowed to open in port. Which is great for me, I can go on the excursions if I want to.'

'How does it work? The shop, I mean? Are you employed by the ship or the cruise line?'

'No, it's like a franchise. Cathy owns it, Debbie and I just work for her, and she pays us. We get the accommodation and food free, so our wages aren't high. Occasionally one of the girls who works in the casino helps out, so that there are always two of us there. There needs to be. You'd be surprised how often we catch someone shoplifting, or trying to. Not all cruise passengers are either wealthy or honest.'

Julie spent an hour wandering through the public rooms, testing the temperature of the water in the swimming pool, gazing at the activity in the harbour from each deck, waving to the people ashore, and then, as the boat finally moved away, returning to her cabin to shower and change for dinner.

'Informal the first evening,' Susan, who had returned to the cabin, instructed.

Julie selected a gored green skirt in a heavy cotton, matching her eyes, and a white lacy top. They were old favourites, in which she felt comfortable. The colours suited her dark auburn hair, and the elasticated waist didn't need pulling tight with a belt as some of her more fitted skirts did. She hadn't bought any new clothes since Andrew's death, until Susan insisted on her getting some for this trip, and she'd been horrified to realise how much weight she'd lost. Swept away by Susan's enthusiasm for spending her money, she'd even splashed out on a couple of what she later felt were far too revealing evening dresses, and even a bikini. She had a moment of thankfulness that she'd packed her old one-piece swimsuit too. As for her new dresses, she'd keep them for when she felt more confident. She added a small emerald pendant, Andrew's last present to her, hanging on a thin gold chain round her neck. It matched her ring and she wore both of them frequently. He'd told her the emerald was the sacred stone of the goddess of love, a symbol of hope and faithfulness.

Susan led the way down a wide, elegant curving staircase to the dining room and they were shown to a table for six. All the crew Susan referred to as auxiliaries, the entertainers, shop girls, musicians and so on, ate with the passengers, and were meant to mingle and act as hosts and hostesses. An elderly couple, both extremely handsome and elegantly dressed, the woman sporting a necklace of diamonds which must, if it were real, Julie thought, be worth thousands, were already there.

'Hello, we're James and Laura Tomkins,' the man said, standing up to shake their hands. 'Your first time?'

They introduced themselves, and made small talk until the waiter appeared with the menu. They had all ordered before the final two seats were claimed, and Julie felt a stab of surprise, and a delight she tried to suppress, when she realised that the newcomer slipping into the seat beside her, wearing a casual but clearly expensive jacket, was the man from the plane, who had carried their luggage to the cabin. Now she would be able to discover who he was, and what his function was on the ship.

'Hello again. Sorry I'm late,' he said easily. 'Don't wait for me, I'll miss the starter. I'm Robert Fellows.'

Before Julie had time to reply, she froze with shock. The final seat was being claimed by another man. He was in his late thirties, with sandy blond hair, and smooth, classical features. He smiled round the table.

'Hi, I'm Steven Wilkes,' he announced. 'I'm so sorry to be late. Let me get the wine tonight as an apology.'

The Tomkins and Robert introduced themselves. Susan, after a swift glance at Julie, mentioned their names. The newcomer smiled across at Julie, who was still rigid with horror. Of all the men in the world, how could this particular one be at their table?

He was speaking again, looking across at her with a self-satisfied smile. Julie felt a sudden urge to slap that handsome face and wipe off that obnoxious grin.

'And of course I know you well, don't I, Julie, my love? Hello there, Susan, good to see you again.'

Julie glared at Susan. Had she organised this? She must have done, it couldn't have been coincidence. How could she, when she knew how he had treated her in the past? A furious swell of anger

21

against both her sister and the man opposite, a man she'd hoped never to see again, threatened to swamp Julie, and she felt sick. She stood abruptly, pushing back the chair. She had to get out of here. As Susan, looking anxious, began to rise too Julie waved her back.

'No, Susan, I'll be OK,' she snapped. 'Don't come. Don't follow me. Sorry, but I must have some air,' she muttered to the others, then turned and almost ran from the dining room.

*

She ran straight up the wide staircase outside the dining room entrance, and pushed her way onto the deck. Without being fully aware of where she went she climbed up to the higher decks, until she could climb no higher. Then she stood grasping the rail so tightly her knuckles grew white, and she found it difficult to breathe. She needed to consider this disaster. And it was a disaster. She was stuck here on this ship for a couple of weeks, unless she demanded to fly home from the first port of call.

Then she stiffened. Why should the wretched man ruin this holiday, as he'd ruined her peace of mind two years ago? She had done nothing wrong, nothing to be ashamed of, and she would not permit him to influence her actions. She gulped in great swallows of air and fingered her pendant, as she often did for comfort. Emeralds were supposed to be calming. She would ask to move to a different table. That would be easy enough. The ship wasn't full, there had been several empty spaces in the dining room. Then all she had to do was make it clear to Steven she had no intention of speaking to him, and hope he would keep out of her way.

There was a sound of someone coming towards her, and she glanced round to find Robert Fellows looking at her, concern in his eyes.

*

Robert's first assumption, when Julie had departed so precipitously from the table, was that she was ill. She had looked so white, devastated, and had been shivering. He felt an overwhelming need to comfort her.

22

'Does she suffer from seasickness?' he asked Susan, pushing back his chair.

Susan was looking across at the newcomer, and both seemed embarrassed, but she shook her head and spoke quickly.

'She's never been on a ship before, but how could anyone feel ill? The sea's like a pond, the movement is barely noticeable.'

Steven coughed. 'I am afraid it was the sudden sight of me,' he said, and smiled. 'We are, what shall I say, old friends.'

Robert doubted it, and found his hands curling into fists. He hastily hid them beneath the table. The man's tone, his complacency, and the smile on his face, which was more like a smirk, made Robert want to hit the fellow. What had he done to Julie? What was he to her?

'What do you mean? Old friends? It didn't look as though she felt that way about you,' he said, striving to keep his voice mild, though his words were not conciliatory.

'I – oh, well, we were once – what shall I call it – good friends? It must have been a shock for her to see me. But I'm afraid we had a rather acrimonious parting, and no doubt Julie blames me. She's never replied when I've tried to explain, make it up, you know.'

He grinned round at the others and picked up his soup spoon as the waiter brought the starters. The Tomkins were looking rather puzzled and turned to Susan.

'Will your sister be all right?' Laura Tomkins asked. 'Ought you to go and see how she is?'

Susan shook her head. She was looking rather flushed.

'It was the shock, as Steven said,' she said. 'It must be difficult to see an old flame unexpectedly. But Julie prefers to be alone when she's upset. I'll see her later, make her have something to eat in the cabin when she'd had some time to recover.'

Robert looked at her for a moment, then rose to his feet.

'Excuse me,' he said, and without further explanation went swiftly from the dining room.

*

'Are you OK?' he asked Julie gently. 'I promised your sister I'd

23

make sure you were all right.'

He hadn't, but what did a white lie matter if it made her more willing to let him help.

She tried to smile as he took her elbow and led her over to some chairs and urged her to sit down. He dropped into the chair beside her and took both her hands in his, chafing them gently.

'I gather you had a shock, seeing him, but you mustn't get cold. Do you want to talk?'

Julie didn't know whether she did or not, but she discovered the human contact was soothing, and the gentle pressure of his warm fingers was a comfort.

'You knew him from before?' Robert asked gently. 'He said something about it.'

'Yes.'

He would, Julie thought. Trust Steven to attempt to show himself in the best possible light, so that afterwards people would think she was protesting too much.

'How did he harm you?'

'Harm me? How did you know? He – well, perhaps it wasn't real harm. It felt like it, to me. But I don't know. He said he'd misunderstood. He – and others – thought I'd made a fool of myself.'

At least she seemed willing to talk, and perhaps telling a stranger would help. He caught his thoughts. He didn't want to be a stranger.

'How long ago?'

'Two years.' Suddenly Julie felt the need to confide in someone. Susan had never understood the remorse she had felt, and would not now. Later, Julie promised herself. Later she'd discover whether Susan, devious and determined to run her sister's life for her, had somehow arranged this. She'd refused to accept Julie's assurances at the time that she never wanted to see Steven Wilkes again, insisting that it had just not been the right time for starting a new relationship, it was too soon after Andrew's death, and later Julie would feel differently.

24

'Tell me if it would help.'

His voice was calm, almost hypnotic. Deep and smooth, confident and persuasive, it made her want to talk to him. His eyes held only concern, no condemnation for her weakness. Julie just knew he could be trusted.

*

Chapter 3

Julie drew a deep breath. She vowed she would be calm, strong. 'It was two years ago,' she said slowly. 'My husband, Andrew, had been dead a year, and Susan persuaded me to go on holiday with her and her boyfriend, and some friends who had rented a villa in Italy. He – Steven Wilkes – was there too, and seemed so sympathetic. I spent a lot of time with him. We were the only unattached people in the group, so we were thrown together. He – assumed more than was there. I just felt he was a sympathetic friend. I wasn't ready for another relationship.'

'He wanted to marry you, I suppose.'

His voice was so matter of fact, and Julie knew she had been making too much of the whole thing, then as well as now. She shook her head.

'It would have been much better if he had wanted marriage. That was what I thought, but – '

Robert squeezed her hands as she forced herself to control her voice.

'What had he done to affect you so badly that after two years, the sudden sight of him unnerved you?' he asked. 'Sorry. Don't tell me if it's too painful.'

Julie shook her head. 'Not painful, shameful. I thought he meant marriage, and I wasn't looking forward to refusing him. He had been kind. But he didn't. He knew somehow that I'd been left quite well off. Andrew had inherited a great deal from his parents, and there was a pension and insurance. He, Steven, made it plain that if I lost some of this income, such as my husband's pension, when I remarried, he wasn't interested. He assumed we could just live together, in my house, and he would have the benefit of my income. I felt – used! Cheap! And a fool for imagining he was fond of me.'

'He's the one who should feel ashamed.'

Robert sounded more furious than she had been, and Julie almost laughed. It meant nothing to him, but his support was

26

comforting.

'I was a fool. I took it for granted when he said he loved me he meant marriage. Perhaps I'm too old-fashioned.'

'No, just honest and normal. But you're not going to let a jerk like him spoil this holiday, are you? The ship's big enough for you to keep out of his way.'

Julie took a deep breath. She had been weak to show her distress, and she was furious with Susan, who must have been behind this. She'd have something to say to her sister later. Meanwhile she was beginning to regain control of herself, able to face Steven, and this man, this stranger, was helping. He was so calm yet strong and dependable.

'No, he'll not ruin it for me. I'd prefer not to meet him, so can I change tables? That would help, not having to see him every evening.'

'No problem. I'll arrange it for you. But he should be the one to move. Now, do you feel able to come back, or would you like dinner to be sent to your cabin?'

Julie looked at him and smiled. He'd helped so much.

'That would let him win, wouldn't it? I was a coward, I ran away.'

'Seeing him must have been a nasty shock. Can you face him? Or shall I arrange a different table now?'

'That would create too much fuss. No, I'll outface him. Thank you, Robert. I'd better go back.'

'I'll be with you.'

*

Julie and Robert went back to the dining room, where the waiter was serving the main courses.

'OK?' Susan asked, looking worried.

As well she might, Julie thought, if her sister had engineered this meeting, and there was no other way Steven could have been on the same cruise, even the same table. Such coincidences just did not happen.

'I suddenly felt rather queasy,' she said clearly, flickering a

27

glance at Steven. 'I'm fine now, thanks.'

She was tired as well as angry with Susan and embarrassed at meeting Steven again so unexpectedly. She'd slept badly and got up at an unearthly hour that morning to get to Gatwick. She ignored Steven, and sat back observing the others.

James was an experienced traveller, commenting on the different ships he'd been on. Steven, not to be outdone, said cruising was a new experience for him, he preferred adventure holidays in exotic locations. Julie was sure, from her earlier contact with him, that he had done nothing more exotic than a week's safari in Kenya. She glanced once at Robert, and had the distinct impression he was thinking the same as he winked at her. She suppressed a desire to giggle.

Susan and Laura were more interested in the shopping opportunities, and what would be good value at the ports on this trip, and what Susan might suggest Cathy bought for the ship's shop. Laura, Julie found, already knew a great deal about several passengers, and seemed willing to gossip about them. Robert, like Julie, sat back and listened, but she was aware that he looked across at her several times. He was so different from Steven, caring rather than self-obsessed.

'Gib tomorrow,' Steven said as the coffee was served. He turned to Julie, a confident smile on his face that made her want to hit him. 'You'll be going up the Rock, I imagine? Unless you've done it before. Perhaps we could make up a party?'

This was something she certainly didn't want, to spend any time with him.

'The boat organises trips, I'll go on one of them,' she said hurriedly.

'They use the same taxis as we can, no monster coaches here,' Steven said cheerfully. 'Costs less by ourselves if we share, the ship doesn't take part of the fare just for arranging it. That's often a better bet, the rate can be negotiated, and we can take all the time we like.'

'How is that organised?' Laura asked.

'They'll be waiting on the quay. So why don't we share one, the six of us?' he repeated.

Julie wondered why she had not seen, two years ago, what a conceited, pushy man he was. Couldn't he see she didn't want to, and what was more, would not be bullied into such a thing? To her relief, before the blistering words on the tip of her tongue could be uttered, James shook his head.

'Sorry, we're visiting some old friends who live here.'

'Then just the four of us? Unless you'd prefer to go up on the overhead rail?' he added, looking at Julie.

'I don't think so. I'm always terrified they'll get stuck. And I'm going on a taxi the ship organises.'

Steven was unrepentant, or oblivious. What an irritating man he was. Why hadn't she realised this when they'd first met, two years ago? Had he been different then? Perhaps, as the people in the villa were his friends, he hadn't felt this pathetic need to impress, to assert himself.

'You won't come to any harm, I promise. There's a wonderful new cable car in Madeira, too, fabulous views over Funchal harbour. I must take you on that one.'

'No, thank you.' Long before they reached Madeira, one of the last stops on the itinerary, she would make it crystal clear to Steven that she wanted nothing whatsoever to do with him. But what she had to say must be done in private, not at this public dining table. Unless, she thought, he became even more obnoxious and tried her patience too far.

'One taxi then. You too, Robert?'

'You heard what Julie said,' Robert almost snapped the curt reply. 'The taxis are ordered, and that's the end of it. Now, please excuse me, I'll skip the rest. I really have to go.'

*

Robert made his way to the penthouse deck, the highest passenger deck on the ship. He nodded to the security guard sitting in the half shadows at the far end of the corridor, and knocked at one of the suite doors.

29

Moments later the door opened and he went inside. A trolley with the remains of dinner on it stood by the door, and he absently helped himself to an apple as he wheeled it outside.

'We can get rid of this and have no interruptions. I see you have coffee waiting.'

A flask and three cups were on a low table. An older woman sat behind the table, and the red-haired girl who had let him in went to sit beside her while he sat facing them.

'Well, young Robert, what are our orders?' the older lady asked. 'What do we have to do?'

He looked at them both affectionately. They had agreed to his plans with no hesitation. Knowing how difficult it might be to catch a thief red-handed, he had devised this plan in the hopes of setting a trap. Even Bea, in the throes of preparing for her wedding, had said cheerfully that she would take the opportunity of doing some shopping.

'Not a lot, Aunt Mary. You and Bea are just passengers, very wealthy ones. No one knows we are connected. Wear as much jewellery as you can, both of you. Be ostentatious about it. Forget about it being tasteful or discreet. We need it to be noticed. The things I provided for you are excellent copies, it would take an expert to tell the difference. Aunt Mary, you are the scatty one, lose your purse as often as possible, forget it, leave it behind, and make a noise while looking for it. Show a lot of cash the first time, then say it doesn't really matter, you'll leave your cash in your suite in future. Bea can complain, say the way you are always losing purses it will be as well if you don't carry cash. And she despairs of how you are always leaving your rings in the bathroom. Use the public loos when people can see you, especially if any of these women are in there.'

He passed over a list and the two women studied it.

'Do we have to swallow this now, like real spies?' Bea asked, a twinkle in her eye.

'Tear it up and flush it down the loo, chief spy!' Robert said, grinning. 'At the public cloakrooms note who follows you in. We think the thief might be a woman.'

'Don't I have to do my Mara Hari act?' Bea asked, laughing.

He grinned at her.

'What would your Jonathan say?'

'We're not married yet, Robert my dear. But I left my engagement ring at home, I wasn't risking your thief getting hold of that.'

'You can make eyes at the single men. They're likely targets too. Start inviting people to drinks, up here, as often as you can. Here's a list of those we want to check up on. Keep it in the safe, you may need to refer to it as there are quite a number of suspects.'

'You haven't taken on an easy job, Robert dear,' his aunt said.

'With your help we'll solve it. We'll keep tabs on which waiters come here, though they are not prime suspects, and after each party we'll check the cash. If it's gone we'll watch the people who could have taken it.'

'We're going shopping in Gib,' Mary said. 'I've been up the Rock before, and we thought that if we arrive back just before the ship sails, when there will be lots of passengers on deck, with as many bags from expensive shops as we can carry, it will establish us as the big spenders.'

'You're not hoping to claim all that back from the company, I hope,' he said, laughing.

'No, it'll be for my trousseau,' Bea said, striking an attitude. 'And I shall, very artistically, drop a bag stuffed with a couple of old dresses over the side as we come up the gangway.'

Robert grinned. Bea had always loved acting, and might have gone on the stage had she not met Jonathan.

'Is this a cue for a great big scene?'

'Of course not. If I did some of you macho men might try to rescue it. I shall shrug, and say as loudly as I can I'll have to buy some more, as I simply couldn't wear anything that had been immersed in such horrid dirty water. The spoilt brat, that's me.'

*

After Robert had departed Steven tried to persuade them to

31

dance, and Susan added her voice, but Julie firmly shook her head.

'Sorry, I'm bushed, I have no wish to dance. I must go to bed.'

Steven seemed inclined to argue, but Susan, after a glance at Julie's face, said she had to be in the shop for a while.

'We had to get up before dawn. Tomorrow, perhaps. Come on, Julie, you need an early night.'

He frowned but bowed to the inevitable.

'See you at breakfast then. Sleep well, ladies.'

Julie was not asleep when Susan finished at the shop and slipped quietly into the cabin. Though exhausted, her annoyance with her sister had kept her awake.

'You arranged this,' she accused as Susan began to undress. 'It was a sneaky thing to do, and I can hardly believe you would hurt me like this!'

'Arranged what?' Susan tried to look innocent as she hung up her dress, and then laughed rather uncertainly. 'Oh, Julie, don't let's quarrel.'

'How could you do this to me? You knew something had annoyed me that last time you tried to pair us off, so how come he's not only on this boat but on our table, and we get thrown together?'

'You liked him when you first met.'

'He was amusing, and he seemed pleasant at first, but I never wanted to marry him – '

'Who's suggesting marriage?'

Julie paused. She'd never told Susan the full truth, that Steven had not asked her to marry him. She'd been too astounded when he'd assumed that, a widow of a year, she'd be only too eager to fall into bed with him and share her home and the substantial income Andrew had left her. She knew that, in her loneliness, and knowing she had to get over Andrew's death somehow, she'd accepted the fact that as the two unattached people in the party they'd been thrown together, but his calculating mind, as he explained the financial advantages of not marrying, had deeply

32

offended her, even though she'd had no thought of marrying him or anyone else.

'Did you tell him I was coming on this cruise?' she asked instead.

Susan went into the bathroom.

'I may have mentioned it. I just happened to see him in London one day while I was shopping,' she said, her voice muffled.

Julie wondered if it really had been as innocent as Susan made it sound, but somehow she doubted it. She accepted Susan was concerned about how long she was grieving for Andrew, but if her sister thought that throwing men like Steven Wilkes in her path was the way to make her overcome her grief, she was utterly wrong.

'I don't want to have to be polite. And I won't to go on this trip tomorrow with him, we'll use the ship's taxis.'

Susan sighed. 'You're making a great deal of fuss, Julie, about nothing. Whatever happened, we're all mature adults, and can surely behave politely to one another for a week or so.'

Julie left it at that. She'd do her best to avoid Steven, but she hoped Robert would be able to arrange for him to be moved to another table. If he couldn't, and she had to sit at dinner with him she'd have to be be polite for the sake of the others, but no more.

*

To her surprise she slept well, the gentle movement of the boat lulling her to sleep. She was wide awake by seven, and she and Susan pulled on jeans and thin sweaters and then climbed to the topmost deck to watch the approach of Gibraltar.

Julie could see why this massive rock fortress was such an important stronghold. It dominated the entrance to the Mediterranean. Whoever had controlled it in the past could prevent enemy ships either entering or leaving the inner sea. She watched the busy harbour, crammed with both merchant and pleasure shipping, and the backdrop of both old and new buildings rising up the steep slopes. They could see the airport on the flat strip to the left, and Julie laughed when a fellow passenger explained that the only road across it, to the entry point with Spain, had to be closed when planes were landing or taking off.

'That must create delays,' she said.

'Not so many as the Spanish customs, who want to examine every car in detail. It can take hours to get through.'

The taxis were waiting on the quay, and people who were queuing were being directed into them. To Julie's secret relief as it came to their turn Robert appeared, dressed in jeans and a grey cashmere sweater. He gave them a reassuring smile, spoke briefly to the driver, and was waiting to climb in after them when Steven, breathing heavily as though he had been running, arrived beside them.

'All set, ladies?' he panted. 'Let me negotiate, or we are likely to be ripped off.'

'The taxi is hired by the boat, at a fixed fare,' Robert said. 'OK, driver, let's go.'

He added something in Spanish which made the driver grin broadly, and move swiftly out of the line, leaving Steven standing alone, looking disgruntled.

The climb, through the naturally occurring caves and the great tunnels carved out of the Rock itself, was awe-inspiring, and the driver explained how holes opened for ventilation had been ideal positions for guns in the great siege of the 1780s. During World War Two the defenders of the Rock had been prepared to retreat into the tunnels and caves if necessary.

At the top of the Rock Susan was enchanted with the baby apes, who looked at her so pleadingly.

'You are asked not to feed them,' Robert warned when Susan delved into her bag for something to give the baby sitting on the wall just an arm's length away.

'I put a banana in my bag from the breakfast buffet. Surely that won't hurt? It's natural food for them, not sweets or chips,' Susan exclaimed and held it out.

The tiny animal took the fruit offered, and to their delight began to peel it. Then, so swiftly they did not see it coming, a large male swung down from the nearest branch and snatched away the banana. Alarmed, Susan stepped back, and almost knocked Julie over.

'Ouch!' Julie staggered, but an arm round her waist saved her from falling. She twisted round, and saw Steven smiling down at her. He must have followed in the next taxi.

'You don't escape me so easily, my love.'

'Julie, was that your foot?' Susan demanded. 'I'm so sorry! Oh, hello Steven.'

'Just the edge of my sandal you trod on, not me,' Julie said. 'It was your crashing into me that almost floored me. Thanks, Steven,' she added reluctantly, and tried to move away, but his clasp tightened.

'Give me a chance to explain, please,' he whispered before he released her.

She did not reply, but made certain she kept well out of his reach as they negotiated the path down to the waiting taxis. Susan has wandered across to a stall selling postcards, but Robert was close beside her. She was thankful for his presence. He helped her in, while the driver, voluble in both Spanish and English, prevented Steven from joining them, as it appeared was his intention.

'No, Senor, sorry, taxi not take more than three. Only three paid for, not four. Go away. I not take bribes,' he said indignantly as Steven pulled out his wallet.

'Never mind, Steven, we'll see you later on, and Julie will dance with you later.'

Julie glared at Susan. She would not under any circumstances dance with Steven. She felt as gauche as a teenager. Andrew had been her only serious boyfriend. They had married when she was nineteen, and since his death the only other man who had touched her was Steven, apart from her father and brother David. Their hugs had been sympathetic, comforting, but Steven's had been different, hateful to recall.

*

Chapter 4

She thought back to that disastrous holiday. It had been just a year after Andrew's death. Susan had insisted she needed to be elsewhere on the actual anniversary, not at home remembering the long, agonising wait when he hadn't come home and she hadn't known what had happened until the arrival of the police. Julie had accepted the sense of this and agreed to go, but her sorrow was still very raw. Steven had found her weeping, in a quiet corner of the garden, on the anniversary, and she'd told him the whole story. He'd been quietly sympathetic, told her his own wife had died recently too, and for a week she had been comforted and grown to like him. He hadn't been nearly as brash and pompous as he was now behaving.

Then he had spoilt it.

'I don't like it, and I will not dance with him,' she said when she and Susan were riding back in the taxi. Robert was in front, talking to the driver, who had some music playing loudly, and there was no way he could overhear. 'You had no right to say I would.'

'Give the poor man a chance to explain,' Susan tried to cajole her. 'All I said was that we'd go to the ballroom tonight. He's told me you misunderstood him, and he's clearly still attracted.'

She'd not misunderstood, she thought grimly, and she could have throttled her sister. Joining them in the taxi, after lingering to buy postcards, Susan had stopped to talk with a disconsolate Steven. She'd been pleased with her promise for the evening, and Julie saw that she was imagining herself as the matchmaker healing some silly, unimportant rift.

'No way will I dance with that creep.'

*

They arrived back at the ship, and while Susan went to help prepare the shop for the opening, after dinner, Julia hung over the rail watching the activity on the quay. Laura Tomkins came to join her and they compared notes on their day, Laura asking how

36

she had enjoyed her trip to the Rock, and telling her about the friends they had visited.

'They do so enjoy living here, but I would prefer somewhere rather bigger if we ever move from England,' she said.

At almost the last minute, when it looked as though the gangway was about to be taken away, a taxi drew up and two women got out, encumbered with a dozen or more bags, some of which seemed to have prestigious names emblazoned on them. Julie, with a slight shock, recognised the red-head who had been on the plane with them.

'They almost missed it,' Laura said. 'I hear they're very wealthy, but I don't know anything more about them. Yet. You can be sure I'll find out,' she added, grinning.

She'd freely admitted she liked gossip, knowing all she could about people around her. Julie hoped that if she discovered the history between herself and Steven she would not broadcast it all round the ship.

'Wouldn't the ship have waited?' she asked. 'They counted us all off, and back, so they must know if anyone is missing.'

Laura shook her head.

'Oh no, cruise ships stick to schedule. If you miss the sailing that's your fault. But from what I've heard that pair could hire a plane to fly them to the next stop. Oh!'

The exclamation was because the younger woman, half way up the gangway, had let go one of the bags, and despite her attempts to catch it, the glossy green and white bag had fallen into the water. The woman looked down at it for a moment, where it floated in the tiny gap between the ship and the quay, then closed her eyes and shrugged, and continued up the gangway.

One of the men waiting to take the gangway down shouted to her.

'Miss, can use a boat hook. We save shopping for you.'

The red-head looked back at him, smiled and shrugged. Her words could be heard clearly by the people on deck.

'Please, don't bother. It doesn't matter. They will be soaking wet, unwearable.'

'It no bother.'

'But I couldn't possibly wear them now, they will be oily as well as wet, impossible to clean properly. It was my own silly fault. I should not have bought so much,' she added, laughing as she continued up the gangway and stepped into the ship.

'All right for some,' Laura said. 'I bet that's a few hundred pounds in the briny. Someone will rescue it as soon as we are gone, a nice present for his girlfriend.'

Julie nodded.

'She didn't seem very worried,' she said slowly. 'She was laughing, so was the other woman. I wonder who they are? I don't recall seeing them last night.'

But last night, she remembered, she had been in the dining room for only a short while before the shock of seeing Steven, and when she returned had taken no further interest in her fellow passengers.

Laura seemed to realise that at the same moment. She patted Julie on the arm.

'Are you OK now?' she asked softly.

Julie smiled at her.

'Yes, thank you. And now, after we've waved goodbye to the Rock, I suppose I'd better go and change for this cocktail party.'

*

The ship sailed at six. Robert had vanished the moment they were back on board, but he'd murmured to Julie that he hadn't forgotten to have Steven moved to another table. It had been clear from Steven's behaviour today that he still thought he would be able to persuade her to forgive him. And what else, she wondered? Did he hope to resume the relationship that had scarcely begun before it had been so abruptly broken off two years ago?

Susan, who had been trying to get her to change her mind ever since she'd come back to the cabin, chuckled. Her voice was muffled by the folds of her evening dress, a floaty concoction in pale pink which she had bought while she was staying in England.

'It won't hurt you to be polite. He's still smitten,' she said. 'Why not? You're a free woman. He's a single man, and even if it was too early for a romance two years ago, surely it isn't now. You can't mourn Andrew for the rest of your life. He wouldn't have wanted that.'

'What Andrew would have wanted is not something you can know, and what I do with my life is my affair, Susan, and I'd be grateful if you'd remember it.'

Susan was unrepentant. 'He's a widower. His wife died five years ago. So you have something in common.'

'Susan, what has that to do with it? I don't like him! I'm not the merry widow! I don't want a man, any man, and especially not him! Andrew was the only one I'd ever love.'

'Rubbish! The lady protests too much. Every women likes some male attention. I'm not trying to marry you off, don't worry. Have some fun. You married Andrew almost out of school, you didn't play the field as I did, and you're not thirty yet.'

Julie chuckled suddenly. It didn't matter, she'd ensure nothing happened this time, and make it crystal clear to Steven that was how it must be.

'I can remember, since we were in primary school, that you seemed to have a different boyfriend every week.'

'Mom despaired of me. Enjoy Steven's attentions. And be glad I'm not jealous. But Robert's attentive too. I was so surprised when he followed you out last night, and when you came back he was so grim-faced. What had you told him?'

'He was kind and sympathetic. That's all.'

She was unsure now why she had confided so much to Robert. She still didn't know what he did. How was he free, if he was part of the crew, to accompany them on a day trip? Was he what Susan referred to as the auxiliary crew, like she was? If so, what did he do, and how did he have the power to get Steven moved to another table? If indeed he had done so. She'd have to wait and see.

She was wearing one of her new evening dresses, and wondering whether to wear a strand of pearls or a silver pendant. Before she could decide there was a perfunctory knock at the door, and it opened. A pretty fair-haired girl put her head round and nodded at Julie.

'Hi, can I come in? Hello, you must be Susan's sister. Welcome aboard. I'm Cathy Smithers, I run the shop, and I came to ask Susan if she can spare me a few minutes straight after dinner, before we open, to look at some fantastic things I bought in Spain. I've only just unpacked them and they're even better than I remembered.'

She stayed and chatted for a few minutes, then left, saying she had promised to meet one of the band in his cabin.

'He's got one to himself, lucky devil,' she said, winking. 'We're going to miss the welcome do. I've heard that speech so many times I could recite it by heart, better than the Captain. See you in the shop soon, Julie, ready to spend lots, I hope.'

She was gone as speedily as she'd arrived.

'So she's your boss, is she?' Julie asked.

'She runs the shop, on a sort of franchise. It's what I'd like to do when I have more experience, but Cathy is not likely to leave, so I'd have to apply to another ship, and I like this one. Besides, I couldn't afford to stock one until I've saved a lot more. I think Cathy had some help from her family.'

Julie glanced at her watch. 'Heavens, it's almost time, we'd better go.'

'No hurry, there's always a massive queue while the Captain shakes hands with everyone.'

*

When Julie, wearing a sheath-like dress in a dusty, blue-grey silk, slit up both sides, was ready Susan led the way to the ballroom deck. Already, though it was not yet the stated time of the cocktail party, a queue had formed outside the ballroom entrance. A photographer was busy taking pictures, and Julie, trying to smile, allowed Susan to pose her in front of the spectacular flower arrangement.

The doors to the ballroom opened, the Captain and what Julie assumed were his senior officers shook hands and murmured polite words of welcome, then waiters handed them glasses of champagne and they moved on to talk with other passengers.

'Look, that's the woman I told you about, who lost some of her shopping,' Julie said, indicating the red-head, who was already surrounded by several men.

'She looks as though she can afford to lose a few designer dresses,' Susan said. 'Just look at those rings the older woman's wearing.'

Julie privately considered the rings, one with an impossibly large emerald to match the older woman's dress, and another, a massive hoop of diamonds, too ostentatious. An emerald necklace dipped tantalisingly towards her cleavage, and several gold bracelets jingled on her arm as she gestured. The red-head wore less jewellery, smaller and more discreet rings, but she had on a complicated necklace like a silver net, displaying many different shades of what Julie thought must be amethysts scattered over it. It almost filled the neck of her evening dress This was almost certainly a designer gown, of shot silk which reflected some of the colours of her necklace. It fitted her perfect figure, and the skirt was a miracle of overlapping petals, again of shimmering amethyst shades. Julie tried not to feel envious. She wasn't short of cash, Andrew had left her better off than many women her age, but she could not imagine how much this gown had cost, or whether she could bear to spend so much on one dress, gorgeous though it was.

They were on the other side of the huge room, talking to a couple of elderly women. These women also sported far too much jewellery, Julie thought, rings, bracelets, and ostentatious necklaces. Then, wondering whether her reaction was just plain jealousy, for her own collection of jewellery was comparatively modest, and all she wore this evening was a single rope of pearls, decided that if they possessed such jewels they were entitled to wear them, to enjoy them, however it looked to others.

The ballroom was crowded, and the small band, which had been playing soft music, suddenly produced a roll of drums. The Captain was now on the stage, and he made a welcome speech, hoping they would all enjoy the cruise, and if there was anything else they needed his crew would do their best to provide it. He mentioned the ports they'd be calling at, and finished by saying they would be at sea on the following few days, and they must relax, and take advantage of all the facilities aboard.

'Oh dear, he will insist on listing them all,' Susan whispered, and just at that moment the Captain's words were lost as a woman cried out that her bag was missing.

'It's slipped from my arm, the strap must have broken,' she cried. 'Oh, where is it? I can't buy anyone drinks if I've lost it!'

There was a ripple of laughter, some people began to explain she could put the drinks on her account, while others nearby began to look under chairs and tables. A moment later a man held up a small, beaded evening purse, and the woman fell on him, gushing her gratitude, and insisting he go with her at once to the bar where she could buy him a drink.

It was the older woman they had been watching, the one with the red-head and sporting the big emerald ring. She opened the bag and held out what Julie could see was a thick wad of banknotes. Susan, beside Julie, hissed in disapproval.

'She ought not to carry so much around,' she said. 'All the cabins have safes, and as they said, everything can be charged.'

Julie was watching the woman, who had been joined by the red-head. She suddenly recalled they had been on the plane, sitting with Robert, though she hadn't seen them on the coach afterwards. Indeed, they had gone somewhere by taxi. Shopping, perhaps? They must have money to burn, though why they had been on a charter flight when they seemed to be so rich she couldn't imagine.

*

To Julie's relief Steven had been placed on a table as far away as

42

possible. As it was that of the Hotel Director, almost as important a man as the Captain, Robert told her with a gleam of amusement in his eyes, he would feel honoured rather than aggrieved. In his place was an older man, introduced at Bill Saunders. He was one of the musicians, and both he and Robert excused themselves before coffee. The others all trooped to the ballroom some time later. Susan said she had few minutes to make sure Julie was settled, before joining the others at the shop when Cathy opened it.

'We're often busy the first few nights, as people try to spot the bargains. Normally two of us manage, but sometimes we need all three.'

Steven was already there, dancing with a young girl who had, Julie thought, a professional smile on her beautifully made-up face. Susan told her she was one of the hairdressers. An elderly man and his wife, Ben and Marjorie Askew, who had been talking to them in the reception before dinner, came across and sat with them. After a few minutes Ben asked Julie to dance.

'Marjorie doesn't dance these days,' he said as he swung her onto the floor. 'She has arthritis too badly. They tend to play the old-fashioned waltzes and quicksteps,' he went on. 'It suits the older customers better, but you're not old enough to know them, I imagine.'

'I managed to stagger round the floor doing a waltz a few times with Andrew, my husband, when he was alive,' she said, swallowing the sudden lump that came to her throat when she recalled being in his arms.

'Follow me, then, I'll guide you.'

Robert passed by at that moment. He was dancing with an elderly lady old enough, Julie thought with surprise, to be his mother. Her raddled face was heavily rouged, her eyes plastered with mascara and eyeliner, eye-shadow a bright blue to match the girlish blue silk dress that was slipping from scrawny shoulders. She wore a heavy necklace of diamonds and sapphires, matching earrings, and there were massive rocks on every finger. Julie

43

wondered whether some of these women brought their entire jewellery collection on cruises, determined to wear them all, getting the use out of them, as her mother would say.

When her partner took her back to her seat Julie saw, to her annoyance, that Steven had joined the group. So had another elderly couple, and Ben began to talk with them.

'Good evening, Julie,' Steven said, a note of satisfaction in his voice. 'Now I've placed your friend, the over-protective Fellows. He's one of the gigolos.'

Julie stared at him in amazement.

'Robert? A gigolo? I don't understand. Surely not!' she said, startled. She'd meant to ignore him, but this was puzzling, and she spoke before she remembered.

Steven laughed. 'Oh, I don't mean a real one, or he'd be sitting on her table. He's a dance host.'

'What's that?'

'Elderly, unattached and wealthy ladies tend to come on cruises. They often like to dance, but there is a shortage of elderly, unattached men on board. So cruise ships employ a few men to keep them happy.'

Julie glanced round. There were a couple more men, older than Robert, but still sprightly and quite good-looking, who were dancing with much older ladies. As the music stopped she watched these men escort their partners to their seats and after a few words move away to ask other elderly women sitting on their own or in small groups to dance.

'Robert's a dance host, but I understand he's new this cruise,' Laura said. Trust her to know, Julie thought, trying not to smile.

'What do they do?' she asked.

'It's normal,' Laura explained. 'Often men who've retired early, are widowed, but still active and able to dance, do it for the company, as well as a free cruise.'

'And the possibility of snaring a rich, doting wife who will soon leave them widowers and well-provided for,' Steven intervened. 'I don't think I'd be willing to take on a woman who's had endless

44

facelifts, like Robert's last partner, even for the financial benefits. Thank goodness I don't have to. My business provides for me.'

'You're a businessman?' Marjorie asked. 'That's such a vague term. What line are you in?'

Julie scarcely heard. Somehow the notion that Robert might be angling for a wealthy, elderly widow was distasteful. She didn't want to believe it. Besides, he was far too young to be retired. So why was he here? Then she tuned back into the conversation.

'Oh, consultancy,' Steven was saying. 'But I come away to forget business, to unwind, so let's talk about something else. Julie, what have you been doing the past couple of years?'

'It's my turn to dance now, Steven,' Laura said briskly as the music started again.

He looked for a split second as though he would reject her, but politeness, and Laura's hand on his arm, urging him towards the dance floor, won. To Julie's relief she whisked him onto the floor as the small three-piece orchestra struck up with a slow foxtrot.

Then she felt a hand on her shoulder.

'Julie? Come and dance.'

She looked up at Robert, and smiled. 'Thank you,' she murmured, wishing her voice didn't sound so husky, so full of unshed tears. She kept remembering Andrew, and all the fun and love they'd shared.

Robert was a superb dancer, much better that Ben, whose style had been energetic and rather bouncy. Robert's style was fluid and restful, yet at the same time sensual. She felt as though she was floating in his arms. Then she recalled his job and stiffened. She felt his hand tighten on hers, and he pulled her closer. Was that his heartbeat she could detect, or her own?

'What is it?' he asked gently.

'Ought you not to be dancing with – ' She halted, embarrassed.

'With unaccompanied ladies,' he finished for her. 'Yes, that's my job, and you're an unaccompanied lady. It's my good fortune you are much younger and more attractive than my usual partners.'

Julie felt a glow of something she had never expected to feel

45

again, gratification at the admiration of an attractive man.

'Do you like your job?' she demanded before she had time to think.

'It's not a permanent job,' he replied. 'They usually employ people for a few weeks at a time.'

'So Steven said. Retired, single men, he said. But you're far too young to be retired, surely.'

She recalled their conversation that first night, on deck, when she'd told him much more than she'd ever told anyone else. How was it that she could talk so openly to this man she scarcely knew?

'I'm not retired. But I am single. I've just taken some leave, to get a bit of sun.'

She had never thought to question whether he was married or not. Somehow her thoughts had not progressed that far. But her heart gave a sudden leap and she tried not to smile. It didn't matter to her, how could it?

'I thought most of you were retired,' she managed, 'Why do you do it?'

He seemed to have money, judging by his excellent clothes. He could surely afford to pay for a cruise.

'For the company? For a free cruise? Ken, that's him dancing with the woman in the silver lamé, and his wife used to go dancing a lot, they even won competitions. He misses that a great deal since she died, that's why he comes on cruises.'

He hadn't answered her question. She thought he was going to add something, but changed his mind. After a brief pause he suggested she told him something about herself, and to her surprise she found herself talking of Andrew more easily than she had done since he died.

'My husband was killed three years ago, a car accident,' she said quietly. Before, she'd just said he had died, not how. 'Susan persuaded me to come on this holiday.'

'I'm sorry, about your husband, that must have been a dreadful shock, to lose him so young,' he said quietly. Did she imagine his arm had grown tighter around her waist?

'Yes, it was, and I still feel angry when I think how unnecessary it was. Just a gang of drunken teenagers.'

'Then it's a good idea for you to have a break, a change of scene. Do you have a job?'

Julie shook her head. 'Well, not a proper job. I make soft toys and sell them to the local craft shops. I married after a year at secretarial college, and then I never had a proper job, as I always wanted to do something where I could be at home. I'd expected to have children, but it didn't happen. Perhaps as well in the circumstances. And my shorthand is decidedly rusty by now. I don't know how to use a computer, and I haven't had the desire to retrain.'

The music had come to an end, and, seeming reluctant, Robert escorted her back to her seat.

'Thank you, Julie. I'd better go and do my duty by some of the other ladies now.'

*

The moment Laura and Steven returned to their little group Julie stood up, saying her legs ached after all that climbing in Gibraltar's steep streets, and announced she was going to bed. As Laura opened her mouth to speak she muttered 'Goodnight' and turned swiftly away, almost running in her haste to leave the ballroom. She was inwardly cursing that she'd made an excuse instead of merely saying goodnight.

'Are you all right, dear? You really disappointed him,' Laura said as she caught up with Julie. 'He was hoping to dance with you at least, and even better to be going for a moonlight stroll on deck with you. He's truly smitten.'

'Nonsense. I detest the man.'

'He doesn't mean any harm.'

'Please, Laura, let it be. I knew him years ago, and I'd rather forget what happened then. He was harmful enough before, and I'm not interested in a shipboard flirtation.'

She hoped Laura, with her penchant for gossip, would not

47

probe, and the older woman seemed to understand.

'I won't be nosy. But it's a boost to know that men still admire you, isn't it?' she said with a slight laugh. 'I noticed Robert watching you when you and Ben were dancing. He seemed less attentive to his partners than a professional host ought to be. Anyway, I must go back. I just wanted to make sure you were OK.'

*

Chapter 5

Susan and Julie took a late breakfast in the deck café the next morning, then Susan had to go to the shop, and after an hour on a lounger, enjoying the sun, Julie decided it was warm enough to swim in the small pool. Several other bathers were already splashing about in it.

Julie had settled for the safety of her old one-piece swim suit, but she admitted to herself that she felt a little dowdy as she contemplated those worn by the other women. Even the rather large ladies wore bikinis, and seemed unconcerned at the rolls of flesh which sprawled unconfined. She still had a good figure, perhaps even better since she'd lost some weight. Tomorrow, she promised herself, she'd give her new bikini an airing. It was green, a colour which always suited her, and not as brief as some up here.

After her swim Julie sat beside the pool drinking coffee. Steven, in shorts and a thin shirt, dropped onto a chair beside her, and put out a hand to detain her when she began to rise.

'Don't run away, please. I want to explain, apologise.'

Julie glanced round and tensed. There was no one else within earshot. Good. Now she could tell Steven a few home truths.

He was beckoning to a deck steward.

'A beer, please. Nice and cold. What about you, Julie? Is it too early for a drink?'

'Nothing.'

They were silent for a while, as Julie considered her best approach, and then Steven, looking serious, leant towards her.

'These dance hosts, like Robert,' he began, 'you need to watch out for them. They are often on the lookout for rich widows.'

She looked at him, scorn in her eyes.

'I'm sure that's not true. And I'm not wealthy enough to tempt someone like that.'

'Any of them could come as ordinary passengers, if they could afford it, so they must be on the make.'

'It's not a crime to be poor, or even less well off than you or I.'
'I'm aware you have a good income,' he said rather ruefully.
'You threw that in my face two years ago. But that's why you need to be even more on your guard.'

'As you discovered, though I now have enough to live on, with Andrew's insurance and pension,' she snapped, 'some of that would stop if I married again, so I'm perhaps not such a good bargain as some people, like you did, may imagine.'

'Don't be mad at me,' he said, laughing. 'I made a dreadful mistake then, but you misunderstood, and didn't give me the chance to explain that I never did need a rich wife. I just don't like handing more to the tax man than necessary. Who does? But I suspect our friend Robert would like someone to support him in style. I think Susan is worried about you.'

'If Susan was concerned about that she'd not have persuaded me to come on this cruise and contrived to get you here too. Steven, for the last time, understand this, as I don't want to have to keep on saying it. I have no interest in you, I don't want your company, or to have you pestering me. I came away to enjoy a cruise, for a holiday, a break, not to have you harassing me all the time. Now I'm going in. We have the lifeboat drill soon, and I need to change.'

*

The passengers all gathered in the ballroom for instructions. Some were already wearing the life jackets, while others carried them, as they listened to one of the crew demonstrating how to put them on, and then directing them to the various lifeboat stations on deck. Other crew members were moving around, helping those passengers having problems. Julie discovered that the straps of hers were impossibly tangled, and while she was trying to sort them out Robert appeared beside her.

'Let me,' he offered. 'Oh dear, someone really made a mess of these. How are you this morning?'

'I'm fine, thanks.'

'Good. I think that's got it. Now pop this over your head.'

She did so, and Robert arranged the straps, in doing so putting both arms round her. She shivered, though it wasn't really an embrace. The bulky life jacket came between them. Nevertheless, the feel of his hands sent goosebumps to her arms.

It seemed impersonal. He didn't permit his hands to linger, as some men would have done.

'Come on, or we'll be late for rollcall.'

He took her hand and led her out of the ballroom, up to the next deck, where they joined a group of people standing underneath one of the lifeboats which was slung up against the side of the ship. Other groups were spread out all along the deck.

The red-head and her older companion were also in this group, Julie noticed, and Susan was at the far side with Cathy. Steven, she was thankful to see, was nowhere in sight. At least if they were shipwrecked she wouldn't have to endure him, she thought with a grin.

She tried to concentrate on the crewman who was telling them what to do should they ever have to use the lifeboats, but all she could think about was the feel of Robert's hands on her arms. They'd been firm, smooth and warm, just like last night when they had danced together. Then it was over, and everyone was dispersing.

*

The shop had been closed during the lifeboat drill, and Cathy was with Susan. They caught Julie up as she reached the cabin, taking her life jacket back.

'Hi, let's go and get a drink on deck,' Cathy said, flopping down on Julie's bed. 'Debbie and Charlotte can cope for a while. Most people will be heading off for lunch. I'll leave the jacket here for now, collect it later.'

On the pool deck they found a table and Bill, from the band, joined them. The red-head and the older woman were sitting at the next table, and Julie noticed that even when she was wearing just shorts and a brief top the girl sported several rings, and the older woman, wearing a simple cotton frock, still had on the big

51

emerald she had noticed the previous evening.

The two of them were leaning towards one another, deep in conversation, and after finishing their drinks they got up to leave. Bill suddenly leapt up, exclaiming. He went to the table they'd just left, and picked up a small black purse under one of the chairs.

'Hi, ma'am, you've forgotten this,' he called, and the older woman turned, glanced at the purse, and came to retrieve it.

'Thank you so much! I'm such a scatterbrain! I'll lose my head next. But I know you, don't I?'

'In the band, ma'am.'

'Of course. You were playing last night. It's a much better band than I expected. How could I have forgotten.'

She smiled round at the three girls, and then looked again at Susan.

'Aren't you from the shop? I have been admiring the selection of clothes you have, especially the tops.' She glanced at Cathy. 'And you work there too, I think? How about you?' she asked, turning to Julie.

'I'm just Susan's sister,' Julie told her. 'Here for the ride.'

'Why don't all of you come up for a drink, before dinner tonight? I expect you can close the shop then? Or perhaps you have other girls to run it. And you won't be playing for the dancing till afterwards, will you?' she added, smiling at Bill. 'I'll expect you any time after six. Penthouse number one.'

Without giving them time to reply she smiled and departed, rejoining the red-head who was waiting further along the deck.

*

Julie found a quiet spot to read for the rest of the day, when Susan and Cathy were busy. As they sailed southwards Steven ostentatiously avoided her, though he did cast a few regretful glances towards Julie when she sat on deck, but did no more than nod briefly when he walked past her. Julie relaxed, and forgot to be on her guard all the time.

She saw Robert once or twice in the distance, but he didn't come near her. He seemed to be devoting himself to a few of the older, single women. Even away from the dance floor, she supposed he had his duties towards the other unaccompanied women passengers. She saw him talking to them, sitting with them on deck, buying them drinks in the bar.

It would have been pleasant, Julie thought rather guiltily, if Robert spent more time with her. Then she told herself not to be stupid, he had a job to do, and even though she was alone now, she had her sister. She was not unaccompanied like these women.

Susan found her at teatime, and said they took it in turns to have time off for meals and breaks, so that they could keep the shop open as much as possible

Julie was unable to resist the delicious small cakes the waiters brought round, and was glad of a cup of tea. It was hotter than she had expected.

'I'll come back with you and see what you have,' she said when Susan said she had to get back. 'I need some more sun blocker.'

*

Cathy was already in the penthouse suite when Julie and Susan arrived, along with at least another dozen people. Julie looked round in awe. Her own cabin was tiny compared with this.

The door opened straight into a sitting room bigger than hers at home. Patio windows opposite revealed a veranda, and to either side she could see through open doors into two double bedrooms. Some of the guests were on the veranda, and the windows from there into the bedrooms were open. The red-head came forward, smiling brightly.

'Hi. I'm Beatrix Talbot, Bea to my friends. I don't think we introduced ourselves. That's my mother, Mary, over there by the window. Come and get a drink.'

A waiter was stationed by the bar in a corner, and Julie found herself clutching a glass of champagne, moving towards the window as more people arrived and Bea left her to greet them. Susan had turned to talk to a man Julie didn't know, and to her relief Julie saw Laura chatting to the elderly woman Robert had been dancing with the previous night. She squeezed past another small group to join her.

Laura smiled, drew her forward and introduced her to the woman, a Lady Jenkins.

'Julie, Lady Jenkins comes on several cruises a year, and she's been telling me the most amazing stories about some of the passengers. Like the American who hired a separate cabin for her dresses. Why she didn't have a suite like this I don't know.'

Lady Jenkins snorted.

'Too mean, spent all her money on gowns that she thought made her look eighteen again, instead of eighty.'

Julie blinked. Lady Jenkins' evening dress, an off the shoulder frilly concoction more suited to a teenager of fifty years ago, made her look older than the seventy-odd years Julie guessed she was.

Lady Jenkins, with the freedom of age and social confidence, began asking Julie about her family, her husband, whether she had children, and where she lived. Appearing satisfied with the brief answers that were all Julie could manage, she gave Julie an approving smile, just as Cathy, with an apologetic murmur, slid past them into the bedroom. Julie, glancing after her, saw her bending towards the dressing table mirror, applying lip gloss.

'I can't think why people have to invite members of the crew to these affairs,' Lady Jenkins said, staring at Cathy, 'nor why the wretched girls can't attend to their make up before they come. Surely no one needs to repair their ghastly eye shadow every five minutes?'

To Julie's relief, before the inquisition continued and she had to confess her sister was part of the crew, they were joined by another couple, and Lady Jenkins turned her attention to them. Julie was able to slip away, and as the window to the veranda was blocked with a group of people, she went through the bedroom and that window, waiting for Susan who followed her, complaining of the crush and saying she needed the bathroom.

Not long afterwards people began to leave. Cathy and Susan,

gathering up Julie, said they must be going, they were due to be in the shop again after dinner.

*

Robert, on receiving the phone call from Bea to say everyone had left, went to the penthouse. Bea and Mary were sitting at the table with Mary's purse open on it.

'Have we struck lucky straight away?' he asked.

Mary nodded.

'I think so. Just a few notes missing from my purse, which I'd left open on my dressing table. But the ring I'd also left there hadn't been taken.'

'Perhaps a trial run, to see if you'd miss them?' Robert suggested. 'A ring would have been missed more easily, but perhaps not notes unless you counted them immediately. So who went into the bedroom?'

'Several people,' Bea replied. 'I kept a check on who went into mother's room, while she helpfully blocked the patio doorway in here. There was nothing left out in mine, so I didn't need to watch that.'

'Who?'

'Mostly passengers we're not interested in, but of the crew, the man from the band, Bill, isn't it? He was on the veranda earlier, but he stepped inside for a minute. To talk to someone, I think, one of the passengers. Cathy, from the shop, went through the bedroom. The other shop girl, Susan, and her sister, Julie, went through to get onto the veranda. Susan went into the bathroom. Julie stopped to talk to someone and blocked my view for a minute or so. The man who plays in the Piano Bar followed them. The dressing table is partly hidden from where I was standing, and from the veranda. It would have been easy to slide out a few notes.'

'Well, unless we have two thieves, we can narrow the suspect list,' Mary said.

'Unless there are two of them working together,' Robert warned, and the others groaned.

55

'True,' Bea said. 'And notes would be difficult to trace. If we'd marked them they'd most likely have turned up in the shop, untraceable. We'll have to wait, tempt them again with the ring. Now I suppose we should go to dinner.'

*

Robert was late to dinner, and seemed preoccupied. Afterwards, when Susan had gone to help in the shop, Julie went to watch a film. She didn't want to go to the ballroom on her own, knowing it would be difficult to repulse Steven if he wanted to dance with her. She suspected he was impervious to her claims she wanted nothing to do with him. Why hadn't she realised what sort of man he was two years ago?

She was having breakfast the following day in the deck café with Susan when Robert, carrying a loaded tray, went past them.

'Hi there,' Susan said, but Robert, with an abstracted smile, simply nodded and walked past to sit at a table at the far end. As they sailed towards the Canaries he was rather distant, less friendly than he had seemed at first. He was amiable enough at dinner, or if their paths crossed during the day, but that was all.

'Have I offended Robert?' Julie asked Susan as she was getting ready for dinner the evening before they arrived at Tenerife.

'Why? What gives you that idea?' Susan demanded.

'He's cold, somehow, not as friendly as he seemed at first.'

'I think Steven may have offended him in some way,' Susan said thoughtfully. 'Haven't you noticed, they deliberately ignored each other when they almost collided, just when they were coming into the dining room for dinner last night.'

It was true, though she hadn't considered it before. Robert seemed to have withdrawn himself. He always excused himself before coffee was served, but that could be explained by the need to be on the dance floor early. It didn't mean he wanted to be away from them.

A small group of people sat together in the ballroom that evening, until the Tomkins, saying they needed an early night, ready for a whole day excursion in the morning, excused themselves. Susan said she must go and help Cathy for the last hour in the shop, and went with them, and Robert went to ask another of the elderly ladies to dance.

Lady Jenkins looked after Susan, a frown on her face, then turned to Julie.

'I wasn't aware your sister was one of the crew?' she said. 'Are you one of the shop girls as well? I haven't patronised it, I find their goods overpriced and poor quality.'

'I simply came on this cruise because I would have company,' Julie said coldly. How dare the old harridan be so snobbish!

'Oh, I see. How odd. Well, please excuse me. I have to go and talk to the Colonel.'

'He's more acceptable than we are, is he?' Steven asked. 'No. don't leave me all alone, sweetheart,' he added, stretching across and catching Julie's hand as she began to get up. 'Come and dance. They're playing a romantic waltz, just the kind of dance we can smooch to.'

Didn't he realise how false he sounded, like some Lothario in a bad film?

'Let go of me, Steven. I'm tired, it's late, I don't want to dance, or have anything to do with you. I am going to bed.'

'But not with me. If it were dear Robert, I don't expect you'd refuse.'

She only just stopped herself from hitting him as she rose to leave. She was furiously angry, both with the snobbish woman who thought she could be rude just because she had a title, and Steven for persisting in attentions he knew were unwelcome, and his insinuations about bed and Robert.

To cool down before she tried to sleep she went out onto the deck and leaned over the rail. The sky was wonderfully clear, full of stars, a sight rarely seen in the south of England where everywhere seemed to be lit up with horrid, harsh street lights. The soft lights of the ship were behind her, muted by drawn curtains over the ballroom and bar windows, and in the far distance she could see another cruise ship with its long line of lit windows. It was truly magical, out here on the sea.

A soft breeze fanned her hot face, and the noises around her, the dance band, the hum of the ship's engines, were so quiet she could hear the slap of the waves against the ship's side. Then she heard the slam of a door, and footsteps coming along the deck, and sighed. She'd been enjoying the solitude, but it seemed it was at an end. She turned to go back inside, but an arm snaked round her waist and she was pulled back against the rail.

'Julie, don't be like this. Give me another chance, and I'll prove to you I love you.'

'Steven! Let me go!' she gasped, struggling to free herself. 'How dare you treat me like this? It's harassment, and how often to I need to tell you I want nothing to do with you?'

'You won't listen to me,' he complained. 'Just because I'm trying to be sensible, minimise our tax liabilities, doesn't mean I wouldn't treat you as my wife. Surely you're not offended by that?'

He pulled her towards him and tried to kiss her, but she managed to twist her face away, though she could not break free of his hold.

'I am offended by you!' Julie retorted. 'I have no desire whatsoever to live with you, whether we were married or not! In fact, you're the last man I'd ever want to live with! I despise and loathe you! You're a creep, a slimy, horrible man! Now let me go, before I scream for help!'

'Bitch!' he snarled, and thrust her away so sharply she almost fell.

To her relief he stormed off along the deck, and Julie, wondering if he had finally got the message, abandoned the deck and went to bed.

She couldn't sleep. To distract herself from her anger with Steven she tried to recall the conversation after dinner when Robert had been so withdrawn. Had there been anything in particular which had given her such an impression, not noticed at the time, but subconsciously nagging at her since? Then she had a glimmer of an idea.

They had been in the ballroom, and Robert, having just danced with Lady Jenkins, brought her to join them when the band were having a break. Steven appeared, and seeming unaware of Julie's frowns, sat down with the group. James and Laura Tomkins were talking of the economy, investments, and whether shares or property would be most profitable in the next ten years. Robert started to speak, but Steven interrupted him, as if his views didn't count. Was that it? There had been a slight stress on his words, 'as a businessman'. Had he been, intentionally or not, putting Robert down?

She hoped not. In fact none of them knew what Robert did. He said he'd taken a few weeks off, but what was his job? He had glanced rather oddly at Steven, pursed his lips and then said no more, listening with an unreadable expression to the rest of the discussion.

*

Chapter 6

Robert went to the Captain's cabin late that night.

'Some notes were stolen, but only a few. As though it was a trial run, to see whether they were missed. I have a list of people who were in that bedroom and could have taken them.'

'It's the same woman who made such a fuss about her bag earlier, and showed how much she carried in it. I hope she is more careful in future. Do you know if she had so much in her bag when the notes were stolen?'

'Yes, she knew, but jewellery would be more positive proof.'

'I suppose so. Well, we asked you here to try and find the thief, so I suppose I'd better accept your advice.'

*

Robert had breakfast in the penthouse with Mary and Bea two days later. They had nothing useful to report. The ladies had held another drinks party, and by now most of the potential suspects had been invited to the penthouse suite, but nothing else had been stolen, despite the many opportunities.

'I've left my purse around and had it returned to me so often I am getting a reputation as a scatty old dear ready for a safe residential home where I can be of no danger to myself or others,' Mary complained. 'I think every passenger on the boat has seen it by now. I've taken off my ring and left it in the loos three times, when one of the girls we suspect is in there, but it's always been returned to me or the Purser. What else can we do?'

'Has anything else been reported stolen? From other people?' Bea asked. 'There are plenty of women here flaunting jewellery.'

'We've heard of nothing,' Robert said.

'What's been the pattern before?' Mary asked suddenly. 'Have these thefts been noticed at any particular time during a cruise? Towards the end, perhaps, when there would be less time for complaint and investigation?'

'Or before a particular port, where they could have accomplices they could pass the jewellery to?' Bea added.

60

Robert shook his head.

'We've looked at all the possible combinations, but there isn't any sort of pattern. Our only chance now is to tempt them to steal the ring and be able to track it.'

'If only we had a clearer idea of who it could be! It might be a man. It's easy enough to take the ring off and forget it when I'm washing my hands in the loo, but that could only trap the girls, and it's beginning to seem as though none of them are guilty. Where else can I take it off, when the men we suspect are around?'

'Most of them are around at some time during the day in the deck café, or in the bar before dinner.' Mary said slowly. 'I have an idea! Robert, can you gather as many of them as you can together. In the bar, I think. You'll have to think of an excuse. Somebody's birthday. Yours if necessary. I will be at the next table. I'll complain my fingers are swollen. Why? I know, I'll have caught my hand in a door. Bea can rush off to find a cold compress, or some ice, the ring can be left on the table, I will feel faint and Bea will escort me off to the cabin. If that doesn't work, we'll have to think of something else.'

Robert laughed.

'Aunt Mary, why don't you write detective novels?'

'Oh, no, dear. Far too much like hard work.'

*

Over the next few days, as they called at several of the Canary islands, Steven appeared to have recovered his good humour. He kept his distance, even when he was on the same coach excursions as Julie, and seemed to have accepted the situation. He was cool but polite when they met, and didn't attempt to stay close to the sisters otherwise.

It was on Lanzarote's Fire Mountain, while they were watching the steam rising from the embers below the hot sand, in the midst of this moon-like landscape created by the volcanic lava, like nothing Julie had ever seen before, that Robert drew her aside.

'Julie, I had a friend check up on Steven Wilkes,' he said quietly.

61

'He's not a businessman, or he isn't now. He was made bankrupt last year.'

She stared at him, shocked. 'You checked up on him? Why? That was a sneaky thing to do!'

Just as Steven had tried to do for him, she thought, from what Susan had overheard.

He shrugged. 'Maybe, but it's clear he admires you by the way he looks at you when you're not aware of it. I didn't want you to be taken in by him, and perhaps get hurt.'

'What I do is none of your business, Robert! I can look after myself, and I have no intention of being taken in by anyone!'

'I was trying to help.'

'Would you like it if Steven poked his nose into your background, checking up on you!'

'He's had a good try, according to what Mrs Laurey told me.'

'Who?'

'Mrs Laurey, the lady with the vast number of rings. She told me he was asking her all sorts of questions the other day, insinuating I was a fortune hunter, and warning her to beware my cunning wiles. We had a good laugh about it. I've known her for years.'

Julie was silent. Susan had seen Steven talking to the old lady, so it was probably true. All the same, she felt humiliated that Robert had felt it necessary, and taken it upon himself, to check up on Steven. She could deal with the wretched man herself, and had. She didn't need the interference, however well meant, of a virtual stranger.

Nonetheless she couldn't stop thinking about it. Was what he said about Steven's financial situation true? And worse than that, did he imagine she was on the lookout for a second husband? But why should he think it when she avoided Steven as much as possible, and made sure they were never alone? Why should he want to put suspicions about Steven into her head? Was he jealous? No, that couldn't be possible.

In time, she admitted to herself, she might have grown fond of Robert. All right, she thought, she was attracted to him already, but she doubted it would have changed into anything warmer. Wouldn't it? A small inner voice insisted that he was the first, the only man to have cracked the hard shell she'd pulled round herself after Andrew's death. Steven had tried, and she'd been flattered for a while, thinking him a pleasant friend, but then Steven had moved too fast, too far, and ruined any remote possibility of her ever becoming fond of him, let alone develop stronger feelings.

She had loathed Steven's attempts to kiss her then, and light though Robert's hugs had been, just friendly embraces, really, she had felt a quiver of long-suppressed desire when he touched her, even if it was only a helping hand. On the rare occasions they had danced together his touch had been impersonal, just as it was when he was dancing with Lady Jenkins or any of the other elderly ladies he was there to entertain. Did that mean she was becoming attracted to him, or just that her protective shell was cracking?

Robert began to talk about something else, and Julie tried to respond normally. That evening, back on the boat, she pleaded exhaustion and insisted she wanted to eat in the cabin.

Susan raised her eyebrows, but to Julie's relief didn't ask questions. She wouldn't have known what to say, and Susan knew her too well for her to be able to give a false excuse. She'd never been any good at lying to her elder sister.

Both Steven and Robert seemed to keep out of her way for a while. She saw Robert only at dinner, when he was polite but distant. Steven, when they happened to meet on deck, which was perhaps too often to be coincidence, would give her a wry smile, perhaps say hello, but he never stopped or tried to engage her in conversation. She was longing for this cruise to end. Enjoyable as the shore visits had been, on board she had not been able to relax. They had two more ports, Funchal in Madeira and Casablanca, in Morocco, and then she could go home and resume her normal life. This cruise holiday had not been a total success, and in future she would resist Susan's bright ideas.

*

Mary and Bea were breakfasting in the penthouse. Both were gloomy.

'I don't see what else we can do,' Mary said. 'I've taken pains to leave this wretched ring on the washbasin in every public loo on board, and I swear it's been there for every single one of the women suspects, and none has touched it except to run after me and hand it back!'

'Robert is beginning to think it must be one of the men. But we'll play out our little plot for this evening.'

'I wondered what you were doing last night, in a huddle with him for so long. His regular partners were looking a bit sour when he didn't dance with them. And that sweet little widow, Julie, was looking wistful. I suspect she has fallen for him.'

'He's been paying her more attention than is wise, unless he's serious,' Bea said. 'In some ways I wish he could fall in love. He's been mourning that girl who died for far too long. I heard a story from Laura about Julie and that creep Steven Wilkes. I'm not surprised she tries to avoid him. But he doesn't seem able to take no for an answer. The past few days he's spent quite a lot of time just looking at her. Though I don't see them talking, he always seems to be in the same part of the ship. I'm not sure if she's aware of it.'

'Well, they'll have to sort it out for themselves. I have enough to do helping to catch this wretched thief. Now, what do we have to do? Give me my stage directions.'

*

'Have a farewell drink with me this evening?' Robert said, as he joined the band members at their table on deck, where they were having an early breakfast. They were due in Funchal within the hour and they all wanted to make the most of this day in Madeira. 'I'm not staying on for the next cruise,' he went on, 'and the last couple of days will be too busy. We leave here at six, so when you've had time to change?'

They nodded and thanked him. He had already rounded up the few other men who had been at Mary's party when the notes had been stolen, and all the male suspects would be in the bar for Bea's little drama to unfold.

*

They were due at Madeira early in the morning, and Julie determined to get up and look at as much as possible of the coastline of what she had heard called an enchanted island. She and Andrew had been promising themselves a visit to see the many wonderful gardens they'd heard about from friends.

'Come on, lazybones,' she urged Susan, but her sister groaned and buried her head in the pillows.

'You go. I've got one of my beastly heads. I'm staying in bed today. But promise me you won't give up going ashore.'

'I'll go, I know you'll only want to be left alone.' Silently Julie dissolved a couple of aspirins in some water and Susan, pale-faced, swallowed the medicine. Julie said no more. Susan often suffered from these debilitating attacks, and only peace and sleep had any effect.

'Lock the door, I don't want anyone barging in. Tell the stewardess not to bother today.'

'I'll come back after breakfast,' she promised softly as she let herself out of the cabin, placing the 'Do not Disturb' notice outside.

She'd see the cabin stewardess later, and despite what Susan wanted, ask her to keep an eye on her sister. And if Cathy was not going on any of the excursions, perhaps she would look in as well. By dinnertime, when the boat was due to leave, Susan might feel like some bland food, but anything now would be counter-productive.

She met Cathy as she was by the deck buffet, helping herself to fresh fruit and a yoghurt. There was so much tempting food laid out, delicious bread and pastries, cold meat and cheese, a variety of hot dishes, as well as cereals and toast, that it was difficult not to gorge. She had, she knew, put on more weight than she wanted.

'Don't worry, I'm coming back on board at lunchtime and I'll look in on her then,' Cathy reassured her. 'She's usually better after a couple of hours, well enough to eat, anyway.'

'The stewardess will have finished, and Susan will have locked the door. But if she's better perhaps she'll open it for you.'

'Don't worry, I know where to find a spare master key. Now excuse me, I'm taking this down to the shop. Things to do while it's closed and before I go ashore.'

Julie was carrying her tray to a table by the side of the boat, from where she could see the rugged coastline coming into view, when she noticed Robert coming towards her.

'May I join you?' he invited, pulling out a chair. 'I've had breakfast, but I need a second cup of coffee. Where is Susan?'

'In bed, she has one of her headaches. She suffers from them occasionally, and nothing helps but to lie down quietly.'

'Have you called the doctor?'

'No, she has pills, and all she needs is rest. But it means she won't be able to go ashore.'

'You won't stay behind with her, will you?'

Julie shook her head. 'There's no need, and it would only fret her. I was wondering whether there's room on one of the trips. We didn't sign up, we were going to explore Funchal on our own.'

'Spend the day with me. I know Funchal quite well, I've been here a few times, and I'd enjoy your company.'

She glanced up at him, and then looked away, flustered by the warmth in his eyes. He had been so cool of late.

'Thank you, I'd like that. We – Andrew and I – always planned to come here one day,' she said quietly. 'I don't know whether I'll feel maudlin.'

'If you want to come back to the boat at any time, you've only to say so.'

'No. I want to see it, for his sake. I chickened out of a whole week here last year, and Susan insisted a cruise was better for meeting people, but if I like it I might come back in a year or two.'

They could see the steep cliffs now, and taking their coffee cups moved to the rail to watch as the boat came towards the great bay which formed a perfect harbour, backed by an amphitheatre of hills, most of them covered with pale-coloured houses.

'Those houses,' Julie said in astonishment. 'Some of them seem to cling onto the hillside with nothing beneath them!'

'The Madeirans are used to steep slopes, their farming in the past was done mostly on narrow terraces. They're great builders, too,' Robert said. 'They build many houses on stilts, perched on ledges too narrow to put a small shed.'

Julie pointed to their right. 'Is that a road, high up over that ravine? It looks impossible! Those pillars holding it up are so tall!'

'The new motorway alternately crosses those deep ravines and tunnels through the mountains,' Robert said. 'Before they improved the roads, only the smallest of cars could manage here.'

Julie watched in awe as the boat came into the port. There were dozens of yachts in the marina, and several other boats moored to the dockside.

'Go and get what you need,' Robert said, 'and we'll meet by the gangway in ten minutes.'

Julie peeped in on Susan, who was fast asleep, and alerted the stewardess, a pretty Spanish girl, who promised to do whatever was necessary.

'Go and enjoy,' she said with a bright smile, and Julie knew Susan was in safe hands.

*

As she and Robert walked down the gangway Julie heard Steven's voice behind her. She thought he was calling her name, but he was too far behind for her to be certain. And surely, after the way she had made it clear she wanted nothing more to do with him, he could not be expecting her to join him on a shore excursion?

There was a crush of people between them, all eager to disembark, and Robert hastened her over to a yellow taxi the moment they reached the dock.

'We'll go to the cable car first, beat the queues,' he said. 'It goes

67

up to Monte. You'll have a wonderful view of the whole town. Then we can decide what to do.'

'I'm not sure I want to, I'm not keen on heights,' she protested, but he reassured her she would be perfectly safe.

'It's an experience not to be missed, it passes right over the rooftops of many traditional houses, and we can see a side of island life not usually visible to tourists.'

Julie allowed herself to be persuaded, but when the time came to step into the small carriage hanging from the overhead cables she refused to sit in the seat next to the window, preferring the centre one. An enormously fat woman followed her in, and Julie was forced to squeeze up to Robert. He put his arm round her and pulled her close.

'That will give you more room,' he said to the woman, but it was clear to Julie that was not his prime intention, and she grinned at his opportunism.

She shrank back as the carriage lifted up above the houses. How the people over whose flat roofs it passed must have disliked it when their privacy was invaded in such a way, she thought, trying to forget about the drop below.

The views were, she had to admit, magnificent, and soon she was craning across Robert's body as he pointed out the various sights. When they stepped out at the end it seemed entirely natural he should keep his arm round her waist.

'I had no intention of going on those wicker sledges, down a steep cobbled street, and depending on a couple of men running behind holding ropes to steer,' she said later to Susan, still amazed at herself for agreeing.

'So was Robert the big protective male?' Susan asked, grinning at her.

'No-o, he just made it sound so ordinary, something anyone could do, that I didn't dare refuse!'

And it had been exhilarating, she confessed to herself, but didn't tell her sister how it had felt to have Robert's arm round her protectively as they sat in the sledge, or how, at one particularly scary moment, she'd turned her face into his chest, and he'd dropped a kiss on the top of her head, and pulled her close.

Back in central Funchal Robert guided her to the old town area. Julie was content to let him organise the day. She knew she would not have time to see more than a small amount, but she'd know whether she wanted to come back.

The market, round an open courtyard, with its massed array of wonderful flowers and all sorts of fruit and vegetables, was almost too tempting. Julie wanted to buy armfuls of the scented blooms, the gorgeous belladonna lilies, the flamboyant strelitzia, and other flowers, but turned away regretfully.

'I can't carry them around for the rest of the day!'

'Have some sent home for when you get back,' Robert suggested. 'I mean to.'

She did that, and then Robert took her to the adjacent fish market, where giant tuna and the long, eel-like, evil-headed espada were laid out on slabs.

'We should have espada for lunch. It's only found here and a couple of other places, because it lives so deep in the sea. Madeira was a volcanic island, and the land plunges as steeply under the water as above it.'

'How do they catch it then?'

'Extremely long lines with lots of hooks. The reduction in pressure kills them as they are brought to the surface.'

They strolled through the old town, had lunch at a table outside one of the restaurants, and then took a taxi to Cabo Girão. It was an enormous cliff, terrifying to stand at the top, but Robert again hugged her to him and she felt no fear.

The taxi back drew into the driveway of Reid's hotel, and Robert led the way to the terrace, where tea was laid out and they could look over the cliff-side gardens and towards the harbour.

'I thought one had to book ahead?' Julie asked, looking at the other tables, all of them occupied.

'I did. I always meant to bring you here today if I could persuade you to join me. It's a wonderful place for a honeymoon,'

69

he added, but so softly Julie could pretend she hadn't heard.

*

'There are so many other places on the island I want to see, Susan, I must come back one day soon,' she said later as they were dressing for dinner.

'We will.' Susan was still pale, but insisted she was quite recovered. 'Cathy made me drink lots of mineral water, and that helped.'

'I want to see the gardens,' Julie went on dreamily. 'You should have seen the enormous poinsettias, growing almost wild in people's gardens. I bought lots of postcards and a couple of books.'

'Perhaps Robert will act as guide again,' Susan said, and winced as Julie threw a pillow at her.

'I'm delighted you're so much better, sister mine. Seriously, is the headache truly gone, and will you be OK for dinner?'

'It wasn't as bad as normal, thank goodness. Now let's go and find a drink.'

*

Chapter 7

Robert was sitting at a table close to the bar, with several men, and didn't notice them come in. Bea waved to them from a nearby table where she was sitting alone, and they joined her. Cathy and several other girls from the crew were nearby, but there were no free chairs there.

They chatted about their day. Bea said they had been shopping for part of the time, for some of the fabulous embroidered tablecloths.

'Though I'll never dare use them, they are so exquisite. You must come up to the suite later and I'll show them to you.'

Just then Mary Talbot came into the bar. She was holding her right hand in her left, and looking rather unsteady. Bea quickly went to her and guided her to a chair.

'Mother, what is it?'

Mary winced. 'It will be better soon, dear. It was the shock. I caught my hand in one of the doors just as it closed.'

'Let me see. It's beginning to swell. Here, take that ring off, or it may be too tight to get off later. I'll get some ice.'

Mary took off the huge emerald ring and placed it on the table, then cradled her hand in the shawl she was wearing. Bea went to the bar, interrupting the barman who was dealing with Robert ordering more drinks, and demanded some ice.

'Can you wrap some in a cloth, please?' she asked, and when he had done so she carried it back to place on Mary's hand.

Mary winced again. 'Gosh, it's cold.'

'It's the best thing for you. But you are looking faint. Come on, we'll have dinner in the suite. Forgive us, girls, but I think I'd better get Mother to bed. No, Mother, I mean it. I'll send for some more ice when we've used up all there is in the suite, and it will be better in the morning.'

She refused Julie's offer of help, but Julie went ahead and held open the door. After they left there was a general move into the dining room. Robert went to the bar, the men who had been with him drifted away, and most of the other people in the bar decided to head for the dining room.

*

Steven was waiting at the entrance to the dining room, looking hurt, and as soon as they appeared he stopped them and demanded to know why Julie hadn't waited for him that morning.

'I called after you, didn't you hear me?'

'I thought I heard your voice, but I didn't hear what you said.' She was rather taken aback by his angry tone. Surely, after what she'd said to him, he wasn't so insensitive to expect her to forgive him?

'I was looking forward to taking you to some of my favourite places. Rosemary, my wife, and I came here several years ago.'

'Things have changed now they've built the motorway, and are building new hotels,' Robert said quietly.

Julie hadn't noticed him come up behind her.

'Ruining the place!' Steven said shortly, and turned his back on Robert. 'Didn't you go, Susan? I didn't see you with this pair, or did they give you the slip too? There were so many dodderers blocking the gangway I couldn't catch them up before Fellows hustled Julie into a taxi.'

'I was in bed, bad headache,' Susan told him. 'Tell me, did you revisit your old haunts?'

'Yes, but it isn't the same on your own. Memories kept intruding, you know.'

*

'I wanted to weep,' Susan said later. She'd left the table after the main course and gone to bed early, and Julie, saying she was tired after the long day, had retired with her. 'As if taking you to his wife's favourite haunts would make you feel sorry for him. I'm beginning to see why you can't stand him. Close proximity hasn't improved him, yet he seemed pleasant enough when we met again in London.'

Julie was brushing her hair until it crackled with static. 'I haven't even been polite. I certainly haven't given him any reason to think

72

I've forgiven him, or want his company, exclusive or otherwise, when we go ashore. Just the opposite in fact. I thought I had finally choked him off.'

'I went up to the deck café with Cathy this afternoon for a cup of tea,' Susan said slowly. 'I was feeling better and peckish by then. He was there, he must have come back early. I was behind one of the pillars and he didn't see me, but he was talking to one of those women Robert dances with, you know, the one who wears all those rings. He was asking her all sorts of questions, whether she knew anything about Robert, had she met him before on other cruises, and so on.'

'What did she say?' Julie tried to sound indifferent.

'I don't think she gave much away. She must be over eighty, but she was flirting with the man!'

Julie laughed suddenly. 'Susan, dear, you'll be flirting with handsome young men when you're eighty, so don't knock it!'

Susan chuckled. 'Not so obviously as she does, I hope. It was nauseating. She actually invited him down to her cabin for a pre-dinner drink.'

'Good for her! Did he accept?'

'I don't know. Someone else spoke to me and I didn't hear. But they'd both gone a few minutes later.'

*

'The ring was taken from the table in the bar,' Robert told the Captain after dinner. 'I didn't see who, and as there were women there too, shop girls and hairdressers, who had been in the suite at that first party, one of them could have stolen it.'

'Then we had better search all of them,' the Captain said, sighing. 'This will be all round the ship in hours, and not do our reputation any good.'

'We can afford to wait,' Robert said.

'But we'll be at Casablanca and they might take it off the ship. It could be they left stealing it until now just because they knew they could dispose of it there.'

'Don't worry. That's covered. I have another suggestion, one that

73

will save too great a fuss,' Robert said. 'There's a tracker device concealed in the setting of ring. That's why we had to make the stone so big! It's a new, specially tiny device, and isn't on the open market yet. The other part which I have will emit a buzz which gets more frequent when we are within a couple of metres of the ring.'

'I see. But why didn't you tell me about this before?'

'Not because I don't trust you,' Robert assured him, and the Captain laughed. 'I just felt it was better that as few people as possible knew of it. You wouldn't mean to, but you might be looking at the ring more than necessary, and alert someone.'

'It's a ring worth looking at!'

'I'll stand by the gangway when people leave the ship, and if anyone is carrying the ring we'll know and can stop them. If no one does take it ashore we can search the cabins of all the suspects. Many of them will have gone ashore. If they have hidden it somewhere else we will have to search the ship until I hear a buzz. We could do that while the excursions are away, it's a long trip to Marrakech, and they won't be back till later than normal.'

*

They arrived at Casablanca very early in the morning. A tour had been arranged to Marrakech, which started out as soon as the ship had completed customs formalities. It was a long drive, over two hundred kilometres, but Julie had decided it was too good an opportunity to miss. Susan had been before, and said she did not feel up to the long day. She'd spend it helping Cathy tidy up the shop ready for the final day before the cruise ended.

Julie was on the first coach, so were the Tomkins, but Steven, she was thankful to see, was on one of the others. Bill Saunders was with them as one of the tour guides. The ship always had at least one guide on each coach, often members of the crew such as musicians or entertainers, but here, Bill explained, there was the senior tour organiser, Gerry King, as well, and a couple of Moroccans too.

'We'll also have local escorts when we arrive,' Gerry King explained as they drove along. 'Now do remember what you were told on the boat, don't display expensive jewellery or watches or cameras, and ladies, if you can put your handbags round your necks and hold on to them in front of you, please do so. And don't stop to haggle with the touts trying to sell souvenirs, keep up with the rest of the party.'

Half way there, after a drive along a desert road where they passed many herdsmen watching over small flocks of goats, they stopped in a small town and went into a café for glasses of mint tea, sweet and delicious. Bill came to join Julie and a few others, and they bombarded him with questions.

'Why do you people sound so distrustful of the locals?' a large American, video camera slung round his neck, demanded.

'You mean the warning about expensive watches and cameras?' Bill asked. 'In one way it's only being courteous, for this is a poor country, and it might breed envy for them to see the sort of luxuries none of them can ever hope to achieve. It's also a temptation to the unscrupulous, who gather in the main tourist attractions. It's much better than it used to be, some years back, when we had to be escorted round the souk with armed guards. One of the guests, then, had his shoulder dislocated when his camera was snatched, and the strap was still over his arm.'

The American looked unconvinced, but his wife clutched his arm and begged him to leave his cameras on the bus.

'You don't want to run any risks, honey,' she said urgently. 'The camera will be safe on the bus, won't it?' she asked Bill.

'Yes, the coach will be locked. You can buy postcards. And remember, if you take photos of the locals, they will expect a small payment. Especially the water sellers, who have a very colourful costume.'

*

They were driven first to Jemar El Fna, the great central square, and Julie looked round her in amazement. There were dancers, snake charmers, people offering freshly squeezed orange juice, nuts, postcards, and other souvenirs. She wandered round in a daze, just absorbing the atmosphere, and then the local guides gathered them all together for a visit to the great souk.

'Best not go on your own, especially the ladies,' Gerry warned, and the Tomkins insisted Julie went with them.

'We have to look after you for Robert,' Laura said, smiling. 'I'm surprised he isn't here to take care of you.'

'Why should he be?' Julie asked, but knew she was blushing.

Once, years before, soon after they were married, she and Andrew had visited one of his army friends stationed in Oman, and she had wandered through the labyrinth of stalls in that souk at perfect ease. Clearly it wasn't as safe to do so here.

The stalls were full of fascinating objects. There were great copper pitchers, delicate silver jewellery, inlaid wooden boxes, embroidered slippers, carpets and wonderful heaps of spices, as well as more mundane electrical and household goods. Laura was in her element, bewailing the fact she couldn't take more than one of the lovely boxes, she just didn't have room in her cases after all the other souvenirs she had purchased elsewhere.

'Whew!' Susan said when they emerged into the open to find the coaches waiting a short distance away across the square. 'I wouldn't like to be there on my own. It is a bit scary.'

'No, it had a very threatening atmosphere. Have we time to buy some postcards?' Laura asked Bill, who had stayed close beside them throughout the time in the souk.

'There's a shop over there,' he said, 'You'll be fine on your own. I need to speak to Gerry about the lunch stop.'

Laura and Julie walked over to where postcards were displayed on a stand. Laura chose a dozen, and a smiling man came up to her, holding a small paper bag.

'You have chosen? A dollar each, please.'

'Thank goodness everyone takes either euros or dollars,' Laura said. 'It makes shopping so much easier.'

She counted out the notes, and he turned to Julie.

'I want to see if they have a guide book inside,' she said, and smiled at him as he turned away.

She chose a book, and handed her purchases to the man behind the counter.

'Five dollars for the book, and four postcards for a dollar. That's seven dollars, please.'

Julie blinked, and handed over the notes.

'Why did the man outside charge me more?' Laura demanded of Bill when Julie told her what had happened and they were back at the coach, waiting to board it.

'Oh dear, another scam, I'm afraid,' Bill said.

Laura fumed, and Steven, who seemed to have transferred to this coach, and was standing nearby, sympathised.

'I wish I'd been there, I'd have sorted him out,' he said, glancing at James.

Did he expect poor James to be standing over Laura to make sure she wasn't ripped off, Julie wondered.

'I know it was only a couple of dollars, but the cheek of it!' Laura complained. 'And he was robbing the shopkeeper too.'

It was soon forgotten, though, when they stopped for lunch, and were escorted towards the restaurant through narrow alleyways. Their local guides, who seemed to have become a whole army of protectors, waved aside the sellers of shoddy souvenirs, urging the tourists not to straggle.

The outside looked unprepossessing, flaking paint falling from a plain, rough wall, but inside was a revelation. The decoration was luxurious, vivid bold patterns on the walls and ceiling, with plenty of gilt and jewel colours. They sat on low couches, Julie managing to dodge Steven and find a place with Laura and James where there were no more spare seats.

They ate delicious spiced lamb and wonderfully fresh vegetables, followed by sweet almond pastries.

'Now for the entertainment,' James said softly to Julie. 'Here come the dancing girls.'

'Just what you like,' Laura said, grinning at him.

It wasn't quite what Julie had been expecting. She had never seen belly-dancing, but the lithe beauty of the girls, their athleticism, the colourful costumes, and the last display by an older woman, who carried a circlet of candles on her head as she whirled, and finally bent backwards until her shoulders were touching the floor, the candles still flickering on her head, was awe-inspiring.

*

'No one carried the ring off the ship,' Robert told the Captain when most of the passengers, those going on excursions and others who wanted just to visit the town, had left. 'The crew at the gangway have a list of the others we suspect, and will bring them to me if any of them try to get off now. Let's get on with the search of the cabins.'

It was an unpleasant task, but Robert was confident he only had to hold the tracker device just inside each cabin to know whether the ring was hidden there.

'This isn't going to work,' the Captain said when they had only a couple more cabins to investigate.

'Well, if we have to trawl through the entire ship, we can still do it before the excursions are back. But then, if it's in a public place, we won't know who hid the ring, and will have to mount a watch all the time to see who tries to retrieve it.'

The Captain groaned. 'That won't be easy.'

'If all else fails we'll use this little tracker on all the luggage as it's taken off, and the passengers too. If we don't find it we'll just have to keep a closer watch on the crew staying on. Some of them will be leaving now, won't they, so if it is still here we'll know the ones that remain are suspects. But I can't see anyone leaving what they must regard as a valuable ring hidden where it could be found when the ship is cleaned.'

The last cabin to be searched was that occupied by Julie and Susan. Robert had left it to the end, convinced Susan could not be the thief, but the ring had not been found anywhere else.

To his horror, as they opened the cabin door, the device he held in his hand began to bleep, and as he and the Captain moved into the cabin, the bleeping got louder and more frequent. Robert, moving as if he were sleepwalking, stepped forward, and the tracker led him to one of the suitcases stored in the wardrobes. He pulled it out and opened it. It seemed empty, but in one of the loose side pockets he found the ring, wrapped in a couple of tissues. He pulled it out slowly, turning it over in his fingers, and switching off the tracker, which was now giving out a continuous bleep.

The Captain pushed past him and lifted out the suitcase. He looked at the labels attached to it.

'Mrs Julie Carstairs,' he said. 'It can't be her, she's only been on this cruise.'

'But her sister works in the shop,' Robert said. He felt numb with shock and disappointment. 'In fact she'll be there now. I assumed she was going to Marrakech.'

The Captain was sitting down on one of the beds, looking triumphant and trying to work it out.

'And Mrs Carstairs might be taking it off the ship with her. But that couldn't have been the method before. They might have used other people, I suppose, or even mailed what they stole. They wouldn't have wanted to trust too many people.'

'Or the sister could have kept everything hidden and taken in to England herself when she had a few days off before this cruise, when you were in port having that overhaul. We'd better put the suitcase back as we found it, and see both of them after dinner. Will you keep the ring meanwhile?'

'I'll put it in the safe, in my office.'

*

79

Chapter 8

Robert could not rest. Surely his Julie, a girl he felt he could love, couldn't be a thief? He had to see her, before dinnertime, before she and her sister were confronted in the Captain's office.

It had been six years since Lucy had been killed, and he had thought then he could never love another woman. He'd seen none to tempt him, until he had seen Julie on the plane, been intrigued by her look of vulnerability, and come to know her on the ship. Was this love? He decided it must be. He'd been tempted to chance his luck and propose when they had been enjoying that magical day in Madeira, but he'd held back, wanting to finish this job, and knowing he could always meet her back in England. Now it seemed providential he had not spoken, if she were concerned with these thefts. He had not felt so devastated since Lucy's death.

*

Back on the coach, heading to Casablanca, James sat with Julie while Laura went to sit with an elderly woman on her own, who had been feeling faint from the heat and the walking to the restaurant.

'I hope you have enjoyed the cruise,' he said, rather stiffly, she felt. 'We hope, when we are all back in England, you will come and see us.'

'I've enjoyed it more than I expected,' she confessed. 'Apart from my dear sister's attempts to throw me and Steven together! She didn't seem to understand I don't want to be paired off, especially not with him! But I think even Susan believes me now she knows him better.'

'You don't wish to be paired with anyone?' he asked. 'Laura has hopes you and Robert might be – what shall I say – becoming friendly.'

Julie shook her head vehemently. James was as big a gossip as Laura.

'I'm not sure if I'll ever be ready for another relationship.'

'Friendship only, perhaps?'

He was silent, and soon snoozing as the coach made its way back to Casablanca.

Could she meet Robert again? Did she want to? She was attracted to him, but she'd thought she didn't want commitment. Yet never to see him again was painful.

In Casablanca, to Julie's surprise, Robert and another man she had not seen before were picked up when the coach reached the centre of the city. They took seats towards the back while driving round to see some of the sights before going back to the ship.

'It's not like the film,' James, who had woken up, said, grinning. 'There's almost nothing of interest, it's a modern industrial city. The main claim to fame is the Great Mosque. I imagine we'll stop there for a few moments.'

They did, and some of the tourists got out of the coach to see it at closer range. Steven came up behind Julie, took her arm, and though she tried to remain where she was, drew her away from the others.

'I need to talk to you,' he said urgently. 'Please, give me one last chance to explain.'

'There's nothing more to say,' Julie said angrily, and broke away from him.

He stepped towards her and she backed away, then felt an enormous jolt as her shoulder bag was snatched by a boy riding pillion on a small motorcycle.

With a cry of alarm Julie stumbled, letting go of the bag, and fell to her knees. Before she could get to her feet Robert, who must have been standing a few feet away, hurled himself at the youths and snatched back the bag, but as he did so he fell and hit the wing of a car following the motorcycle.

The car sped off, leaving Robert lying, dreadfully still, in the road. Julie scambled to her feet and flung herself down beside him, frantically feeling for his pulse, and looking to see whether he was bleeding. His trousers were torn below the knee, but to her enormous relief there was no blood, and no splintered bones jutting out at odd angles.

81

'Robert, oh Robert, darling, are you all right?'

He opened his eyes and took a deep breath, looking up into her eyes.

'Say that again,' he ordered.

'Let me get to him, young lady, I'm a doctor,' one of the other passengers said, and Julie, only now realising what her words had revealed, allowed herself to be pulled back.

Robert sat up, pushing away the doctor and handing her bag back to Julie.

'Thanks, I'm fine, just winded. The car barely touched me. I'll have a bruise tomorrow, and my trousers are ruined, but no worse. Now, let's all get back to the ship.'

'And your wife can look after you.'

Julie looked guiltily at Robert, blushing.

He looked at her, but he wasn't smiling. Perhaps he was more hurt than he was admitting.

'Sure, that'll be the best medicine, cure me in no time, Doc.'

To her relief Gerry made him sit on the front seat, so she was unable to speak to him during the short drive back to the port, and Gerry escorted him on board before any of the other passengers. Laura was full of concern, wanting to know whether Julie had been hurt, but fortunately neither she nor anyone else but Robert had heard those incautious words. What had possessed her? She'd been so frightened, seeing him lying there, frightened he was badly injured, like Andrew, and she suddenly knew she didn't want to lose him.

*

Julie tried to push the thought of what to do out of her mind during dinner. Robert wasn't there, and she worried his injuries had been worse than he tried to pretend. Perhaps even now he was in the small hospital suite, being treated, perhaps having gashes sewn up. She couldn't eat a thing, and when Laura, concerned, asked if she felt ill, said she must have eaten too much of that delicious lunch.

Laura looked sceptical, but to Julie's relief didn't comment.

82

Susan was quiet, saying her headache was threatening to come back after a whole day sorting out stock and checking what they had left, but Cathy needed help in the shop with the last minute rush before the cruise ended.

Afterwards, Laura persuaded Julie to go with them to the ballroom for the nightly show, and listless, knowing she would just worry about Robert until she saw him again, she agreed. Robert might be there. He could have had dinner in his cabin.

As they left the dining room, though, Robert was waiting. To her relief he looked normal, though rather pale, and he didn't smile at her. But he wasn't limping, so perhaps he was all right. He came alongside her, took her arm, and said the Captain wanted to see her and Susan. He turned towards Susan, and ushered them along one of the passages into a lift, and it took them up to where the Captain had his office next to the bridge.

*

Mary and Bea had dined in the penthouse with Robert. They had not been on the excursion, but as soon as he had showered and changed out of his torn trousers he'd dressed in his dinner jacket and gone to tell them the ring was found, and where.

'That pretty widow? I don't believe it!' Bea declared. 'No, Robert, it's not her.'

'It could be her sister, but as Susan will be remaining on board, Julie must know about the ring if she's planning to take it back to England. God knows, I don't want to believe it, but how else can it be explained?'

'And I'd so hoped you had found someone,' Mary said softly. 'It's high time you forgot Lucy.'

Robert was silent. He'd been thinking about Lucy more than usual of late. She had been killed in a train accident six years ago. It had been just a month before their wedding, and he'd thought he would never forget her, never get over his loss. Despite the urgings of his relatives and friends, he had never before wanted to take anyone else out. Then he had met Julie, and something about her, her gentleness, her quiet beauty, the sadness in her eyes when

83

she thought no one was looking at her, a sadness which mirrored his own, and above all a desire to protect her from such boors as Steven Wilkes, had broken through the carapace he'd erected round his emotions.

Now it seemed she was a thief, or at least an accomplice to one.

He listened to Bea fiercely defending Julie, and trying to find reasons for her to be innocent, but he could not believe in any of them. He dared not hope. She would be convicted, there was no excuse.

'I must go and find them, take them to the Captain,' he said at last. 'Don't, Bea, the evidence was there. They must be guilty.'

*

The Captain invited them to sit on chairs facing his desk, and indicated the one beside him for Robert. It looked like some inquisition, a court where the accusers faced the accused, Robert thought.

The Captain had the ring ready in a drawer of the desk. He produced it, with what Robert sourly regarded as an unnecessary flourish, and held it out on his palm so that the girls could see it.

'Why, isn't that the ring Mary Talbot wears?' Julie said, smiling and turning towards Robert. 'She'll be so pleased it's been found.'

Then, as neither of them responded, she looked puzzled, and glanced from him to the Captain's unsmiling face.

'What is it? Why have you asked us here?'

The Captain turned to Robert, eyebrows raised, but Robert shook his head. He simply could not bring himself to tell Julie, let alone accuse her.

The Captain shrugged, and turned back to the girls, twirling the ring in his hand.

'This valuable ring,' he began, 'was today found in your suitcase, Mrs Carstairs. Can you explain how it came to be there, hidden in a pocket, wrapped in tissues?'

Julie had gone so white Robert thought she was about to faint, but she grasped the edge of the desk and took a deep breath, shaking her head. He could have sworn the production of the ring

84

had shocked her, but was it the shock of discovery, or of innocence?

Susan, in contrast, had flushed, but it seemed like anger rather than the embarrassment of being found out.

'What right have you to search our things without permission?' she demanded, so furious her words were tumbling out of her mouth. 'Are you accusing Julie of putting it there? That's utter and complete nonsense! She wouldn't steal a – oh, I don't know! An apple fallen from a tree onto a public path! She didn't put it there, and if you are thinking of accusing me, I didn't either! Oh, how dare you! I won't stay on this ship a moment after we get to Malaga, and if you don't apologise I'll find the best lawyers to demand compensation for this libel!'

'Slander,' the Captain said, and then recalled himself. 'I think you are protesting too much, Miss Phillips. No one else can get into your cabin – '

'Apart from the stewardess!' Susan interrupted.

'Are you accusing her?'

'No, but what you said is wrong. She can get into the cabin, and perhaps someone else crept in while she was, I don't know, fetching something or answering someone's bell. Or perhaps she left the door unlocked. The people on board might have suspected you were searching the ship, and dumped the ring.'

'Why should anyone else hide this stolen ring there? How could they hope to retrieve it later?' the Captain asked. 'And why would they want to hide it anyway?'

'How the devil do I know?'

'We were searching, someone might have known that,' Robert put in, and the Captain gave him a glance of irritation.

'As soon as we arrive at Malaga the local police will be called, and you will be arrested,' he said. 'I will have you escorted to your cabin now. It will be as well for you if you stay away from the other passengers and do not attempt to speak to anyone of this.'

He glanced at Robert, then rang a bell on his desk. When one of the officers came in he asked him, without any explanation, to escort the ladies to their cabin.

'Are you going to lock us in, add false imprisonment to what we'll be charging you with?' Susan demanded.

'You will be free to use the ship's facilities as normal,' the Captain said, 'but it is late now, and I doubt you will want to talk to anyone else tonight.'

Julie cast an anguished glance at Robert, and he started up from his chair, wanting both to assist and comfort her, but the Captain pulled him back.

'Let them go,' he ordered.

Julie managed to rise to her feet, and Susan, spitting mingled curses and threats of what she would do if the Captain's accusations were not withdrawn, put her arm round her sister and together they walked from the office, followed by a somewhat puzzled officer.

Robert, with just a nod to the Captain, swiftly left also. He could not endure any further discussion.

*

Susan, who often resorted to sleeping tablets, insisted on giving one to Julie.

'I'm so angry I won't sleep a wink,' she raged. 'Nor will you, so although I know you don't like them, you must have one tonight. How could he! And Robert just sat there, believing we're thieves! I thought he liked you, in fact I – but never mind that. Here, take this.'

Numb, Julie did as she was told. She undressed in a daze, but when she was in bed, and Susan was asleep, she still lay sleepless. How had that wretched ring got into her suitcase, and why had anyone put it there? When would they be hoping to retrieve it? She would have been packing on the next day, her suitcase would be on its way.

Then she recalled what Susan had told her. The suitcases would be placed outside the cabins on the final night, and the crew would take them to a central point from where they would be unloaded straight to the quay, ready for passengers to reclaim on

86

their way home. Could someone have been hoping to break into her suitcase and retrieve the ring while it was there? The case was locked, but it would be comparatively easy for anyone with a picklock to open it, even perhaps to close it afterwards, so she might never have known how the case had been used.

Why should anyone do such a thing? And how had they got into the cabin? When?

It was always possible the stewardess had left the cabin unlocked, but she had seemed honest and careful. Might she be the thief, or in league with whoever it was? How could she have stolen the ring, if she had? The stewardesses did not go to the public rooms, where she might have had an opportunity of stealing the ring, but others of the crew who might have been in league with her could have done.

Julie recalled the previous night, when Mary had taken off the ring because her finger was becoming swollen. Had she left it on the table in the bar? Might one of the barmen have found it? Had they persuaded the stewardess to hide it, in case they were suspected when the ring was missed and Mary remembered where she had left it?

No one else could have got into the cabin except by chance. Could it be someone who occupied one of the nearby cabins, taking a sudden opportunity. Yet why should they, unless they were afraid of being suspected of the theft?

Why should they? OK, the ring had disappeared, apparently after Mary had left it in the bar. But surely only the people who had been present would know it was there, unless a complete stranger had walked past the table later and seen it. Had Mary been complaining while many of the passengers were in Marrakech? If so, the thief had to be someone not on that trip.

She turned over for the tenth time. Why didn't Susan's pill work on her? She looked at the luminous dial of her travel alarm. Only half past two. Another four hours at least until she could reasonably get up and wander onto the deck.

Suddenly she recalled Cathy saying she could get hold of a

87

spare master key. If she could, perhaps others might know how to as well? She'd talk to Cathy in the morning. On the thought she fell asleep, and when she woke it was after nine in the morning. Susan had gone, leaving a note on the dressing table to say she was in the shop, and suggesting they didn't mention the accusation to anyone else.

'I'm sure it will all be cleared up today,' she'd finished, and Julie could only hope she was right.

*

Robert sat up all night, trying to think of ways in which the ring had appeared in Julie's suitcase, and reasons why she could not be a thief. When the midnight buffet was well over, he went out on deck, and sat on one of the deckchairs beside the swimming pool, hoping the cool night air would help him to think this through. It didn't help, and after an hour, feeling chilly and wishing he had thought to bring a thick sweater out with him, he went back to his cabin.

Julie wasn't a thief, he was now prepared to stake his life on that. But was Susan? Had she planned this without Julie's knowledge? He knew so little about the sisters, just what he had been told by them.

Suddenly galvanised into action, he went back to his cabin, collected his laptop, and took it down to the ship's computer room where he found another man surfing the Internet.

First he sent a stream of emails to the office, marking every single one urgent, to be answered as soon as possible. Then he began to search. There would probably have been press accounts of Andrew's death, especially since he had been young to die. It had been in a car accident, he recalled, about three years ago.

It took an hour, but he found the details, a small Coroner's report, but after all that effort it didn't add anything to what he already knew. Julie had a big insurance lump sum, as the other driver had been drunk and held totally responsible. She also had a pension from his employers. Googling her name came up with an article on the toys she made, and there were some enchanting

88

illustrations, but nothing more. Susan's name generated nothing, there were several Susan Phillips, but none of whom seemed at all like her.

It was six before he went back to his cabin. He really ought to try and snatch a few hours of sleep, and maybe in the morning he would have some more ideas. He had to find a way of exonerating Julie, his love, the woman he was now sure he wanted above everything else, to marry.

*

Julie knew she couldn't face anything to eat, so after a quick shower she dragged on jeans and a thin sweater, and went to the shop, which was busy with passengers making last minute purchases.

Susan saw her and came across.

'Are you OK? You were so fast asleep I didn't want to disturb you.'

'I'm fine now, but your pill didn't work for hours. I need to speak to Cathy. Can you ask her to come outside for a minute? I don't want to have to talk to her in here.'

Susan looked at her, puzzled.

'Why?'

'Susan, please, I'll tell you later. Do as I ask, I haven't a lot of time left to clear our names, and Cathy might be able to help.'

Her sister shrugged, but nodded.

'As soon as she's finished with that customer.'

Julie retreated. There were some big, comfortable sofas in an alcove just outside the shop and she sank down into one. She hadn't really planned what she meant to say, but hoped inspiration would come.

It was ten minutes before Cathy appeared and sat down beside her.

'What is it, Julie?' she demanded. 'It's bedlam in there, you can see how busy we are, I can't afford the time for a cosy chat.'

'Did you go into my cabin yesterday?' Julie asked. 'Did you hide that emerald ring there?'

89

'What? Julie, have you gone mad? What emerald ring? Why do you think I know anything about an emerald ring?'

'That monster one Mary Talbot wears. She lost it yesterday, left it in the bar, and you were at a nearby table. Everyone heard about her swollen finger, and that she took the ring off.'

'So what? There were a lot of people in the bar, I recall. I didn't take any notice, I was talking to some of the girls.'

'You know how to get into my cabin. And the ring was found there, it had been put there while I was out yesterday. I don't believe Susan did it, or the stewardess. That leaves you.'

'What? That's ridiculous! Only you and Susan have keys, and if you are insinuating I took hers yesterday you're quite wrong.'

'No, I'm not saying that. But you told me, when Susan was ill, that you could get hold of a spare master key. Perhaps you still have it?'

Cathy stood up and glared at Julie.

'You are mad! I can borrow a master key from one of the stewardesses, yes, but I didn't yesterday. You can ask them. Now are you going to apologise? I'm amazed a sister of Susan could be so crazy as to suspect her best friend of stealing, let alone trying to compromise you by hiding the wretched thing in your case!'

'How did you know where it was?' Julie demanded, standing up and facing Cathy.

For a moment the girl looked blank, then she laughed.

'I was guessing. Where else might a thief hide something small like that. If there is a thief, and you have not just made it all up for some odd reason. Now I have to get back to work. I don't have leisure to concoct fairy stories like the leisured classes do!'

*

Robert, who had been about to join Julie on the sopha, had stepped back behind a big potted palm when he saw Cathy come out of the shop and walk across to her. He hadn't been able to hear everything, but he'd heard enough to realise that here, perhaps, was the solution to the mystery. He turned round and headed for the computer room.

An hour later he was in the Captain's office.

'My people back in England have checked out what I discovered,' he said. 'Cathy Smithers was convicted of theft three years ago and had a few months in Holloway.'

The Captain blinked hard and shook his head.

'She had impeccable references,' he said.

'We both know references can be forged. Did you check them?'

'I was in a hurry to get a replacement to take up the franchise, after the previous shop owner collapsed with a heart attack. So young too.'

'So you didn't check.'

The Captain shook his head.

'Are you absolutely sure?'

'My staff are. When she came out of prison she changed her name and her family helped her start this shop. I imagine they wanted her out of England, they are quite a well-known clerical family and as an ex-con she would have been an embarrassment to them.'

'I'd never have thought it. She seems such a nice girl.'

'I suspect she has been keeping low for some time, but recently the urge to sample the pickings on board must have overcome her. I suggest we look at her shop's accounts too, while we are about it. Or get the accountants to check. I'll be busy elsewhere. She somehow has access to a master key and has been known to get into Julie's cabin, visiting her when she was ill. Can you send for her now?'

The Captain sighed.

'I suppose I'll have to.'

He rang the bell on his desk and gave orders, then sat with closed eyes while they waited. Robert remained silent, offering up thanks that Julie would now be exonerated. He just hoped she would not hold it against him, or believe he had for a moment suspected her.

*

91

Chapter 9

Julie was walking on deck, wondering what to do, whether anyone would believe her about Cathy, when Steven appeared by her side.

'Almost over,' he said, falling into step as she paced along the promenade deck. 'I can't say it has been a success, from my point of view. I'd hoped to see more of you, hoped to get you to change your mind about me.'

He seemed subdued, and for a brief moment Julie felt sorry for him, than she hardened her heart. This was perhaps a last ploy to soften her.

'No, Steven, I won't do that,' she said. 'Now, please excuse me, I have to go and speak to someone.'

He caught her hand.

'Please, Julie, just agree to see me occasionally, for a drink, a meal, nothing else. After all, we are both single, and I'm lonely, I expect you are too. We could be company for one another.'

Did the man never give up? Julie shook her head in amazement.

'No,' she said again, more forcefully.

She pulled away from him, and darted through the nearest door. Who ought she to speak to? Somehow she did not want to go to the Captain with her suspicions. He probably wouldn't believe her, he'd already made up his mind she was guilty. She heard the door opening behind her, and fearing it was Steven leapt into the lift beside her just as the doors closed. She couldn't go down to her cabin in case he followed her. She wouldn't put it past him. She pressed the button for the penthouse deck before she had thought it through, then smiled. She would go and tell Mary and Bea her theory and see whether they believed her. If they did, perhaps they would go with her to the Captain to explain, and surely he would believe them.

*

Cathy was brought to the Captain's office, angry and belligerent, but when confronted with the evidence Robert had collected, she broke down in tears and admitted the temptation to steal the ring, lying so forgotten on the table in the bar, had been too much for her.

'Why did you try to throw suspicion on Mrs Carstairs?' Robert asked.

'I was afraid,' she sobbed. 'I didn't mean to get her into trouble, I thought she probably wouldn't find the ring. And if she did, she wouldn't know how it got there. People often don't use those internal pockets in cases.'

'What did you mean to do?' Robert asked.

Cathy had no spirit left.

'I knew you'd search, and as I'd been in the bar I'd be suspected. I had the master key, I could get into any cabin on that deck, but I know where Julie lives, and I could go there later on, after the next cruise, perhaps, find some excuse, and get the ring back. I've a few days' leave after the next cruise, I meant to go to England.'

Robert looked at her in disgust.

'What else have you stolen? Apart from the money from Mrs Talbot's purse when she had that party you went to her in her suite.'

Cathy looked at him in alarm.

'How did you know about that?'

'Never mind. You admit it?'

'Just a few dollars. The purse was open, and she wouldn't miss them, she's rolling in money.'

The Captain frowned.

'What about the things that were stolen on previous cruises?' he demanded, taking a list from a drawer in the desk. 'Look through these and see what we know about. Of course, there may be other things people didn't report, but if you admit to it all perhaps the punishment will be less severe.'

Cathy went pale, and barely glanced at the paper he handed over. Suddenly she sighed and sat up straight.

'OK, if I admit it, will you let me go? I promise I'll never do anything like it again.'

'It's a disease,' Robert said slowly. 'Will you promise to go back to your family and get treatment?'

Her eyes lit up.

'Yes, yes, of course, I'll do anything so long as I don't have to go to prison.'

'I can't guarantee that, but perhaps your family will speak for you, take you in hand.'

'What about my shop?'

The Captain glanced at Robert.

'What can we do about that? The stock belongs to Miss Smithers.'

'Then I suggest we buy it from her, and employ Susan Phillips to run the shop. But you, Miss Smithers, will be escorted back to England, you won't be free to disappear and change your name again.'

She paled and gave him a hunted look.

'How do you know I did that?'

'I have my methods,' he replied, feeling like a ham detective in a third-rate drama. 'I know you were in prison, too.'

She made no more protests, submitted to being locked in a secure cabin near the bridge, while the Captain made arrangements for her to be escorted to England. He sent the Purser and two of his assistants to close the shop and make an inventory, and Robert was finally able to escape. He must find Julie, but before that he would let his aunt know the thief had been caught.

*

The Talbot ladies greeted Julie warmly and when she told them she thought she had discovered the culprit they insisted she join them for lunch in the penthouse while she told them all about it.

'So you'll get your ring back,' she finished.

Mary laughed. 'That trumpery thing. I shall be glad not to have to tote it about any more. You didn't think it was valuable, did you?' she asked, seeing the puzzlement in Julie's eyes. 'None of our jewellery is real, just good copies. We couldn't risk anything valuable being stolen, and perhaps not recovered.'

94

'Though you could trust Robert to find it,' Bea put in.

'Dear boy. He's my nephew,' Mary explained. 'We came with him in order to try and find this thief who has been making a nuisance of herself for several months. I'm not really as scatty as I seem, leaving my purse and that dreadful ring all over the place. We were trying to tempt the thief.'

Julie swallowed hard.

'I see,' she said, though there were a hundred questions she wanted to ask these amazing ladies. 'You believe me then? Will you help me to persuade the Captain?'

'There's no need. Robert apparently overheard your conversation with Cathy, and he did some research on the Internet. I haven't a clue how, but apparently he found out things about her that convinced the Captain, and she has confessed.'

Julie breathed a sigh of relief. She didn't have to try and convince anyone of the girl's guilt.

'Robert is your nephew?' she asked, latching on to this other surprise.

'Yes, and we are so proud of him. Once we suggested we might help, he thought up all sorts of traps we could lay, but none of them worked until the ring was stolen.'

'How did they find it in my case? Did they search everyone's cabins? It must have taken a lot of time, surely there couldn't have been enough just while we were on that trip to Marrakech?'

'Robert has a device, a tracker, I think he calls it, and the other part of it was attached to that ring. When he got near the ring it bleeped, so all they had to do was poke it into cabins until it gave a signal,' Mary explained. 'He can tell you all about it later if you are interested in these things. I just about understand they work, not how!'

Julie had been thinking back to some of the things which had puzzled her during this cruise.

'You lost something in Gibraltar,' she said. 'It fell over the gangway rail. You had such a lot of shopping.'

'Oh, that,' Bea said, laughing. 'It was to imply we were so

wealthy we could afford to lose things. To tempt the thief. I had a designer bag prepared with a couple of old dresses, it didn't contain anything new. I hope if one of the men on the quay fished it out he wasn't too disappointed. As for the rest, I'm taking the opportunity to shop for my trousseau. How old fashioned that sounds, but when I get married I want lots of madly beautiful clothes.'

'You're getting married?' Julie asked.

For a moment her heart almost stopped. They were cousins, but cousins could marry. Surely Robert was not going to marry this girl? But why not? She was beautiful, and lively. Then Bea spoke again.

'Jonathan, my fiancé, will be meeting us at Malaga. He's got a villa further along the coast, and we're staying there for a couple of weeks, to recover from the exhaustion of playing these parts. Perhaps, one day, you'll come and visit me there?'

Julie gulped. 'I'd like that,' she managed. 'Now, perhaps I'd better go and do my packing. We have to put the cases outside the cabins tonight, I understand.'

They didn't try to detain her, and she spent the rest of the afternoon folding and re-folding her clothes. She wondered where Susan was, but didn't feel ready to go up to the shop in case Cathy was still there. What would they do to her? Did they have prison cells on cruise ships?

*

Susan didn't appear till it was almost time to go down for dinner. She was bubbling over with excitement.

'Guess what, it was Cathy all the time, she put that ring in your case, and she's confessed. And apparently she has a record, she's been in prison!'

'How do you know?'

'The Captain sent for me and asked if I was willing to take over the management of the shop. He had to explain why. They will buy the stock, that's what we've been doing all afternoon, calculating what it's worth, and I will be employed by the cruise

96

line. It won't be a franchise any more. I couldn't afford that, anyway, there's thousands of pounds tied up in the shop.'

'How – how wonderful!' Julie said, pleased for her sister. 'But Cathy was a friend. Aren't you shocked?'

'Huh! What sort of friend would try and lay the blame on my sister? Let's go and get a drink, and celebrate.'

Everyone on the table had heard rumours, and Robert told them briefly what had happened. Susan was congratulated on her good fortune in being promoted, and both sisters on being freed from suspicion. James ordered champagne, and Laura said they must all come and visit them some time.

'When you next get back to England, Susan, make Julie bring you. And you, Bill, I think you were under suspicion for a time, from what Robert says, just because you were at that drinks party.'

*

As they left the dining room, planning to go to the theatre for the final show, Robert slipped his arm round Julie's waist and steered her towards the door opening onto the deck.

'Come outside with me for a few minutes, I have some things to ask you,' he said.

'There are lots of questions I want to ask you,' she said. 'You didn't explain the half of it in there. I've been talking to your aunt and cousin.'

'I know, they told me. I only missed you there by a few minutes. But here is a better place.'

He led her, his arm still around her, to the stern of the ship where they leaned over the rail and watched the silvery wake spreading out behind it.

'How did you get involved in detective work?' she asked.

'I work for the shipping line.'

'As a gentleman host? But – I thought you said the ships didn't employ hosts on a permanent basis?'

'No, that's not my job. My company owns freighters and container ships, but we are expanding into cruise ships. I have been learning the ropes, you might say, seeing how everything is organised. It's only on this cruise I've been a host. I've been steward, barman, waiter, even a chef, during the past few months, trying to judge the sort of people we need to employ in order to have an efficient operation. But for this job, trying to find out who was stealing from passengers, I had to be closer to them, so being a host gave me that opportunity.'

'I see,' Julie said slowly. He must be high up in the company to be doing such an important task, for she had seen that the whole comfort of the passengers depended on the quality of staff employed.

'So can we meet back home?' he asked.

'Is England your home?'

Julie knew she was prevaricating, was frightened of commitment. On the one hand she would miss his company, but she didn't want to become too involved, of giving him the wrong impression.

'My home is in England. Only a few miles from your house, in fact.'

'How – I suppose you looked at the ship's records!'

'I did. Now, how about answering my question? Can we meet occasionally? For a meal, friendship, nothing more threatening.'

Julie took a deep breath. She liked him, he was pleasant company, but would he keep it that way, or would he be like Steven, and expect too much of her?

'Can I tell you later?'

'Sure. There's no hurry.'

They talked of other things, and Robert amused her with stories of the crazy things that happened aboard cruise ships, most of which were never seen by the passengers.

'I don't want to pressure you,' he said at last, 'but I know I want to see much more of you, Julie. I hope you meant what you said. Could you, one day, love me as I love you?'

She was startled, but found a thrill somewhere deep inside her. She didn't want to lose him, so she had to be brave.

'How – we've only known one another for a couple of weeks.'

'That's long enough. I was attracted to you on the plane. You looked sad, somehow, and I wanted to kiss away the worry and the strain I could see. I know why, now, but I'm willing to wait until you're ready for me.'

Julie took a deep breath and turned towards him. She had to let go of the past. 'I didn't know, until you were hurt. I thought I couldn't face another relationship, not yet, probably not for years, but when I thought I might have lost you, it was different. And when I thought you might believe I was a thief, I was devastated.'

'Can you love me?'

She took a deep breath, then nodded. He pulled her into his arms, tilting her chin so that he could kiss her lips.

'If you knew how badly I've wanted to do this,' he murmured softly into her hair when he finally let her go. 'Can I hope that one day you'll be ready to marry me?'

'I think I'm ready now,' she said, surprised at herself, and the utter certainty she felt.

'I'm not after your money,' he said, laughter in his voice. 'I wasn't quite honest with you, the shipping company belongs to my family, so I don't need a rich widow. And I have never been married, though I was once engaged.'

'What happened?' she asked, for his voice had softened.

'She was killed in a train crash, six years ago, just before we were to have married. I never found another woman I wanted to spend the rest of my life with, until I met you.'

It was some time later before they went back indoors, into the bar where Susan and Mrs Laurey were sitting with the Tomkins and the Talbots.

'Where have you been?' Susan demanded. 'You weren't in the cabin. I wanted you to celebrate with us.'

Robert had beckoned the waiter and quietly ordered bottles of champagne. Julie looked at him in sudden trepidation. This was such a big step, and a holiday romance at that, but when he smiled at her she knew everything would be all right.

'Drink to us,' he said as the waiter poured the champagne into flutes. 'Julie and I hope you'll come to our wedding, as soon as we can arrange it.'

The cries of astonishment and delight attracted the attention of the other people in the bar, and as they raised their glasses Julie caught a glimpse of Steven, a look of fury on his face, swinging round and pushing his way out of the bar. She didn't have to think of him any more. That was all finished with. Robert she loved, and could trust, and she was impatient for the cruise to end, so that they could begin their life together.

***

THE END

Marina Oliver has written over 80 novels, all are now available as Ebooks.
For the latest information please see Marina's web site:
http://www.marina-oliver.net

More Ebooks by Marina:

A QUESTION OF LOVE

Pippa, an American, wants to prove to her protective family that she can stand on her own feet. She is reluctant to return to the States after a few months in England and do as they and her father's partner expect, marry the partner's son Frank.

Defying Frank, she accepts a job in Minorca as secretarial assistant to a former film star who is planning to write his memoirs. These promise to be explosive, and both his last wife and his nephew Juan try to persuade him to abandon the idea.

*

CHANCE-MET STRANGER

Janie Tempest's idyllic cottage, left to her by her godmother, is being demolished to make way for a new industrial park, and at the last minute the removal company can't do the job of moving her large items.

Luckily the men dealing with her neighbour's move are willing to help.

The handsome Manuel asks her out for dinner, and then becomes involved in her feckless sister's latest disaster.

To make things even worse, Brian, the step-nephew of her godmother produces a will leaving the cottage to him.

*

ISLAND QUEST

Ros Farleigh needs to find her half-brother. Tim Preston, nineteen and on his own for the first time as he works his way round the Mediterranean, playing the drums in hotel bands, vanished three months earlier leaving his precious drums behind.

Always a regular correspondent, his last letter was full of mysterious hints of danger, surprises, and secrets. His last few postcards from Majorca had been marked, indicating isolated coves and unidentified buildings.

Ros is staying at the Castilla hotel from which Tim vanished, where she encounters Lorenzo y Carreira, dark, arrogantly Spanish, talented guitarist, and too handsome for his own good.

Sparks fly. Tim had mentioned going sailing with Lorenzo, and he might be able to help.

Ros begins to learn some puzzling facts.

*

Fatal Slip

The first Dodie Fanshaw mystery

Flamboyant, wealthy, middle aged and several-times married Dodie Fanshaw is in Madeira to help make a film about her early life as a chorus girl and Hollywood starlet, and her husbands.

She is not amused when her son Jake, indifferent actor, appeals to her for money. Instead of going back to England he remains in Madeira and contrives to alienate Dodie's friends, a rival actor, the Madeiran family who run the hotel where he had been staying and a wealthy elderly woman with whom he is now living.

The situation becomes intolerable when Jake, drunk and abusive, comes uninvited to a party on a yacht on New Year's Eve, arranged to watch the annual Funchal firework spectacle.

***

23535625R00059

Printed in Great Britain
by Amazon